Bravely YOURS

AJ RANNEY

Rudy House Publishing

Bravely Yours

A Half Moon Lake Novella

Copyright @ 2024 A.J. Ranney

Line, Copy, Proofreading by Beth Lawton at VB Edits

Cover by Taylored Designs

ISBN: 979-8-9890878-4-6 (ebook)

ISBN: 978-1-965124-00-0 (paperback)

❀ Created with Vellum

To anyone who needs to hear this:
You are worthy of happiness.
Be brave enough to accept it!

Listen on Spotify!

Nothin' Like You - Dan + Shay

Stronger (What Doesn't Kill You) - Kelly Clarkson

Wait in the Truck - HARDY, Lainey Wilson

Heart Like A Truck - Lainey Wilson

5 Foot 9 - Tyler Hubbard

Next Thing You Know - Jordan Davis

Am I Okay? - Megan Moroney

Sky is the Limit - Mark Ambor

Last Of My Kind - Shaboozey, Paul Cauthen

feelslikeimfallinginlove - Coldplay

Girl Like You - Jason Aldean

Please Please Please - Sabrina Carpenter

Somebody's Problem - Morgan Wallen

Prettiest Girl I Don't Know - Troy Cartwright

Everything He Couldn't - Chase Matthew

Behind Blue Eyes - Limp Bizkit

Ever the Same - Rob Thomas

No One - Alicia Keys

Chapter One

SARAH

"I UNDERSTAND THIS IS HARD, but keep your head down and don't do anything stupid."

Would packing our crap and fleeing in the middle of the night be considered stupid? Probably. But at this point, that idea wasn't completely off the table. I didn't want my ex anywhere near my baby girl.

I blew out a breath. "Like what?"

"Like don't lock the baby in the car. Stuff he could use against you."

I glanced over to the purple Pack 'n' Play in the living room area of my apartment. It was supposed to be a safe place for my one-year-old daughter to play, but instead, it became the cage she screamed from any time I put her down. Tonight, she'd fallen asleep early, so I'd gotten a reprieve from the tears while I cooked dinner. Hopefully I'd get a good six-hour stretch out of her, especially since she was asleep in her crib, which rarely happened.

It wasn't fair. None of it was. The gift of a child shouldn't be given to someone like Drew. All I could hope was that his time in jail had changed him. But what if it hadn't? What if he hurt Nora? How do other parents handle these situations? I'd almost lost her once because of him. The thought of her being hurt was twisting my insides into knots.

"Sarah?" Elliot's voice brought me back to the conversation. "The restraining order is in place, as well as all the stipulations regarding how the supervised parenting time will go." A rustling noise came through the line, like he was shifting. "You won't need to see each other, and his probation officer, as well as the social worker, will be there the entire time he's with Nora. Remember, the court only granted him thirty minutes twice a month. I know you're nervous, but trust me, this is actually the ideal situation."

I huffed. Nothing about this was ideal. But there was only so much I could do. No way would I go against a court order, and although it was tempting, I wouldn't run. I'd grown up in this small town. My parents lived here. I loved my job as a kindergarten assistant. But to protect my daughter? Disappearing didn't seem completely unreasonable.

"I'll be in touch once the parenting time is scheduled."

"Okay."

After I hung up with Elliot, I blinked down at my phone for several seconds, replaying the conversation. When the baby monitor on the kitchen island crackled, I let out a long sigh.

Reluctantly, I made my way down the hallway to my bedroom and quietly pulled the door closed behind me. If she was just stirring, I might be able to soothe her back to sleep without picking her up.

I stood in front of her crib, gently rubbing her back, then jolted when a loud beeping echoed through the apartment. I craned my neck toward the door.

What the hell was that?

Ugh. Whatever it was would definitely wake Nora.

Wait.

Was that the smoke detector? My stomach sank. I had been pan-frying chicken on the stove when my lawyer called. Crap. I'd totally forgotten about it.

Nora pulled herself to stand, sleepily rubbing her eyes, then reached her chubby arms out to me. With a soothing shush, I picked her up and rushed back toward the kitchen.

Halfway down the small hallway, I was slammed with the acrid smell of burnt chicken. It was followed by a banging noise so loud I almost jumped out of my skin. Either someone was knocking on the door, or the grumpy old man who lived in the apartment above me was stomping.

Great. Just flipping great. Whoever it was would just have to wait.

As if the sounds and smells weren't chaotic enough, Nora joined in, letting out a wail. I froze in place at the mouth of the hallway, overwhelmed, as the thick smoke drifted through the air coming from the small kitchen. How had it gotten this bad so fast?

How could I be this dumb? Not only had I forgotten about the food on the stove, but now I was holding my one-year-old and didn't want to take her into the kitchen filled with smoke.

Nora would just have to cry it out. At least she would be safe in her Pack 'n' Play. More banging echoed through the apartment, startling Nora and making her cry harder.

"Hold your suspenders, you grumpy old man. I'm working on it," I screamed at the ceiling as I deposited Nora into her Pack 'n' Play so I could deal with the burning chicken. Then I needed to open the windows and take Nora outside until the smoke cleared.

The dark, dense smoke wasn't good for anyone, let alone a baby. And the last thing I needed was for the fire department to show up and insist we go to the emergency room to be checked for smoke inhalation. But with the way that these loud, obnoxious alarms were still blaring, that was exactly what would happen.

Wouldn't that just round out this shitty night? Ironic, when my lawyer just said *don't do anything stupid*.

Chapter Two

JAY

Two weeks. That's exactly how long it had been since I'd had a full night of sleep. As much as I wanted my own space away from my parents and two younger sisters, this was not what I'd imagined it would be like when I agreed to sublet an apartment from my friend Owen.

The all-night crying had been enough to have me pulling my hair out, and now this.

I was standing outside my neighbor's apartment in nothing but a pair of gym shorts. The door vibrated against my fist as I banged hard on it for the third time. Intuition was telling me that something wasn't right. At twenty-five, I was one of the youngest guys at the fire station, but my dad liked to remind me that I had been born with instincts that made me a good firefighter. Apparently, it was ingrained in the men in our family, a trait passed down from one Mitchell to another.

I wasn't sure about all that. But I couldn't deny that my gut was screaming at me. Between the smoke detector and the wailing baby—not that the crying was new in this apartment— something was off. This wasn't a fussy baby. This one sounded scared.

As I stepped back once again, waiting for my neighbor to answer the door, a thin stream of smoke billowed out from under the door.

Shit.

My training took over then. I stepped back, lifted my foot, and kicked hard at the doorknob, praying she didn't have the damn thing dead-bolted. Thankfully, the lock disengaged, and the door swung open.

Instantly, smoke wafted into the hallway. Visibility wasn't terrible, but a thick band of smoke came from the kitchen. My guess would be some type of cooking oil. Depending on which type, burning oil could easily create a lot of smoke. And very quickly.

I turned one way, then the other, taking in my surroundings. The baby stood, crying in some type of play pen. The plastic box off to the left could hardly be called a crib. The sound of coughing from the kitchen area caught my attention. Through the smoke, I could just make out a tall woman standing by the window.

"Fire department," I called out, hoping I wouldn't frighten her as I came around the island and into the kitchen. But between the loud alarm and the baby crying a few feet away, I wasn't sure she could hear me. As I moved closer to her, I surveyed the stove, and my shoulders relaxed a fraction. There was no fire, and she'd already turned off the burner.

"Is this stupid thing glued shut or what? I swear this shit only happens to me. Just wanted a nice quiet night," she rambled, grunting and tugging on the window that wouldn't budge.

Although I was annoyed with the situation, I couldn't hold back the smirk and the snarky remark on the tip of my tongue. "Yeah, me too."

The tall blonde jumped and spun to face me with wide eyes. Her face was stricken with fear. Though, for a second, I was sure her gaze dropped down to my bare chest. I hadn't really pictured my neighbor as I cursed the crying night after night, but if I had, I would not have envisioned a beautiful young blonde.

She coughed again, and the baby echoed the same sound from a few feet away.

I stepped toward the gorgeous, frightened woman. "Move, please."

"What?" She shook her head, her brows furrowed.

"Move so I can open the window and let some smoke out."

With another cough, she stepped to the side. Quickly, I took over and yanked the window up before I moved past her to slide the patio door open.

The baby coughed again, sending a niggle of worry up my spine. I turned and studied her quickly, then focused on the blonde. Her eyes were still wide as she surveyed the front door, then squinted at me.

"Did you just break into my apartment?" Her green eyes narrowed, but the crack in her voice ruined the tough-girl stance.

"Technically," I hedged, rubbing at the back of my neck, "yes."

She turned suddenly, putting herself between me and the baby, then hurried over to the crib.

"I said 'fire department' when I came in, though." I crossed my arms in front of my chest. She was acting like I'd broken in to do her harm rather than to help her out.

She spun again, her brows almost to her hairline. "The fire department is here?"

The woman and the baby coughed in unison, and worry pulled at the corners of the blonde's mouth.

Dropping my arms, I shook my head. "No. Just me."

I took a step toward her, concerned about her breathing as well as her daughter's, but as I did, she startled and took a matching step back.

She was a skittish thing. Or maybe I was just an asshole dressed in nothing but gym shorts, who'd broken into her apartment and scared the shit out of her. Regardless of my intentions, I needed to get her and her baby out of here. And probably give Owen a call. They should be checked out. "I'm Jay. I live in the apartment next to you."

"Oh." Her shoulders relaxed a bit. "You moved in a couple weeks ago, right?"

Nodding, I slowly moved toward the door and waved for her to follow me into the hallway. "Come on, let's go to my place. My buddy Owen is a paramedic and lives in the building around the corner. I can give him a call to come check you two out."

"We're fine." She shook her head. "That's not necessary."

The baby coughed into her shoulder, and I cocked an eyebrow.

"Okay." Her body deflated, and she let out a sigh. "Just to be sure Nora's all right." Pulling the baby closer and cradling her head, she shuffled out into the hallway in front of me.

Once I'd gotten the woman—Sarah—and the baby settled on the sofa in my living room, I stepped away to call Owen. As

I went, I snagged my T-shirt from the back of the chair, where I'd discarded it earlier. I'd been getting ready to jump in the shower when the smoke detector went off next door.

I tapped Owen's name in my recent call log and slipped the T-shirt over my head. I had just brought the phone to my ear when the call connected. "Hey, need a favor."

"What's up?"

"There's a woman here with a baby—"

"Yours?"

I scrubbed a hand down my face and groaned. "No, asshole. It's the one next door who cries all the time."

He chuckled. "What do you need?"

"They need to be checked out for possible smoke inhalation." I glanced over to where the two sat on my sofa. "The woman almost burned her apartment down with a pan on the stove. Can you come?"

"On my way."

Five minutes later, Owen stepped through the door. Living in the same apartment complex came in handy sometimes, though tonight, his presence rubbed me the wrong way. I couldn't figure out why it did until the third time Sarah lit up with a smile at something he said. That's when it hit me that I wanted that gorgeous smile aimed at me.

Sarah

. . .

"Both mom and baby sound fine." Owen leaned forward and tickled Nora's belly, causing her to squeal in delight.

This guy was so good with her. He was going to make a good dad in a few months. As he'd looked us over, he'd gushed about his girlfriend, who was five months pregnant, and he'd gone on and on about how he couldn't wait until their daughter was born.

"Just follow up with her pediatrician tomorrow morning." With a smile, he stood.

Even as my lawyer's words rang through my head, I nodded. One wrong move, and Drew could argue that I was an unfit mother. The court would never give Nora to a convicted violent offender, though, right?

"Of course," I said, holding Nora a little tighter. "Thank you again."

He nodded and then headed toward where Jay stood near the front door. The two guys were an unlikely pair. Owen had worn a smile since he walked in and had happily chatted throughout his exam. Jay, on the other hand, hadn't stopped scowling. Almost like he was annoyed that we were here. He was the one who'd invited us over, so I didn't get why he thought he had a right to be irritated.

But now that we'd been given the all-clear, we could head back to my apartment. The smoke should have cleared by now.

"Thanks, man." Jay clasped hands with Owen and slapped his shoulder, promising to follow up if anything else came up.

After Owen left, I headed for the door, ready to get out of Jay's way. As I approached, he shut the door behind Owen and spun, almost colliding with me. He threw his arms out and grasped my shoulders, steadying me. The warmth of his palms heated my skin through the thin fabric of my top, and a fluttering moved through my stomach.

The scowl he'd sported for the last twenty minutes morphed into something sexier, though it didn't even remotely resemble a smile. A vision of his muscular chest from earlier and the way his shorts hung low on his hips floated through my mind. Man, this guy was gorgeous.

"Thank you." I smiled, dipping my head. "You know, for breaking in and checking on us."

"Of course."

The deep rumble of his voice was doing stupid things to my body.

Get a grip, Sarah.

His lips turned up slightly, and holy hell, he was even more sexy when he smirked. I'd probably need a cold shower if he donned a full-on smile.

He brushed his hands down my upper arms, and I had to fight the urge to sigh. How long had it been since I'd been touched like this? Was I that deprived of physical affection?

"Let's go take a look at your door." Lowering his hands, he stepped around me. A moment later, he returned with tools in hand. "If I can't fix it tonight, I'll at least make sure you can close it and secure the dead bolt."

Without waiting for a response, he stepped out into the hall.

I spent the next twenty minutes trying and failing to not ogle the man. His forearms and back muscles flexed as he worked, and I chastised myself each time I found myself staring.

After he left, my body was lit up in ways I hadn't experienced in years. Even using my favorite toy in the shower later that night wasn't enough to satisfy the hunger that had consumed me. Instead, it left me only semi satisfied and feeling stupid for fantasizing about my young neighbor.

I had to get it together. Right now, the last thing I needed was to be distracted by a hot guy.

Keep your head down and don't do anything stupid. Elliot's words ran through my mind again.

He was right. If I screwed up, there was a good chance it would cost me my daughter. And that was one loss I'd never be able to live with.

Chapter Three

JAY

FORTY-EIGHT HOURS LATER, any carnal thoughts of the gorgeous blonde and her smile had been replaced with annoyance. I'd only gotten a few hours of sleep last night. Again. Nora could stand up, so she had to be around a year old, right? Didn't babies that age sleep through the night?

I was a pro at braiding hair, and I knew all the best filters to use on TikTok. I could even take a perfect selfie, thanks to my two younger sisters. But babies? I didn't have the first clue.

And it didn't help that I was on shift today. It had been a

relatively busy day, thank fuck. For as exhausted as I was, I gladly welcomed the adrenaline rush. But did it make me an asshole for being thankful for emergencies? Maybe.

I scoffed. The guys were all scattered around the firehouse. The crew from the next shift were filtering in, and a few of the guys from the current shift were finishing a game of rummy.

"Still not sleeping?" Owen asked as he stepped up next to me.

Side-eyeing him as he poured himself a cup of coffee, I grabbed my full travel mug and pushed away from the counter. I had twenty minutes before I was off. Then I needed to stop by the grocery store before heading home.

"No." For the life of me, I didn't understand how he'd functioned when he lived there. "Didn't all the crying keep you up?"

"I was at Cece's more than I was at my place." His brows pulled together. "I really don't remember the baby crying a lot when I was there." He chuckled. "But I can sleep anywhere, through anything."

A lot of the guys here were like that. It was a great skill in our line of work, but it was one that I didn't possess. Maybe someday I would, but right now, I still needed a dark, quiet room to fall asleep. Sleeping at night wasn't the only issue I was dealing with. Each evening, the crying started a little after six p.m., so I couldn't even relax at home.

"Lucky you," I mumbled. "Cece will love that when the baby comes."

He shot me a smirk. Lately, he'd found my disposition quite entertaining. Most of the guys did. Assholes.

Even my loud, chaotic sisters didn't drive me nearly as nuts as this baby had in the last few weeks.

Maybe, eventually, I'd get used to it, but thirty minutes later, as I made my way down the coffee aisle in the grocery store, I was sure that would never happen.

Because as my cart rolled across the waxed floor, crying broke out in a nearby aisle.

"You've got to be shitting me," I mumbled. Jesus, not here too. Was I imagining the crying? It was pretty likely, since it was all I heard anymore. I turned the corner and instantly froze.

Sarah was halfway down the aisle, standing on her tiptoes. Her shirt rose high, showing off inches of creamy skin as she reached up to grab a can off the top shelf.

I was mesmerized, but only for a moment before Nora's cries brought me out of my trance, the shrill sound sending a shudder down my spine.

"Mommy's right here. You're fine." Sarah shook a toy that made a rattle sound.

With a frustrated grunt, her little girl swatted it away and reached out.

"Can't hold you right now, baby. Need to finish our shopping." A sigh left her mouth as she moved her cart forward. She'd made it a couple of feet before she looked up and locked eyes with me.

Nora was wailing again, and before I knew what was happening, my feet were moving. I couldn't take it anymore. If it wasn't used already, the sound of a baby's cry could easily be utilized for wartime torture.

"Here." I reached out. "Give me the baby."

Eyes widening, Sarah pulled the cart back. "What?"

"You're disturbing the peace."

She lowered her brows and hit me with a glare. "Excuse me?"

"If she wants to be held, then I'll hold her while you finish your grocery shopping." I huffed out a sigh. "Anything to stop the crying."

As Nora studied my face, then my outstretched arms, like she didn't mind, I suddenly wondered what I'd volunteered for. When she batted at me with her pudgy hands, I swallowed hard, then scooped her up. Instantly, she stuck her thumb in her mouth and laid her head on my shoulder.

"See? How hard is this?"

Sarah fisted her hands on her hips. "Maybe it wouldn't be so difficult if I had a second set of hands. But I can only do so much on my own." She pushed her cart past me. "But since you so kindly offered." She rolled her eyes. "Feel free to carry her while I finish my shopping."

Wet, slimy fingers hit my face, and I cringed. What had I gotten myself into?

Chapter Four

SARAH

THIS GUY WAS KIND of a jerk.

Apparently, Nora and I had the same taste in men, because she was eating up his attention. I had to hold back laughter at the way he cringed each time she took her hand out of her mouth and touched his face. On top of the separation anxiety we were battling, my poor girl was teething. Going back to work full time in August after a summer off had been an adjustment for both of us.

"Um," Jay said from behind me.

I spun and chuckled at his grimace. The expression screamed *What is going on?* As Nora continued to gum on his shoulder, I fought back laughter.

"She's teething." I shrugged. "It's either your shoulder or your finger. You decide." Spinning back around, I continued forward, hiding the smirk on my face.

The young guy probably had zero experience with babies. In fairness, when I was in my midtwenties, I didn't either. But now, as I was approaching thirty-two, my life had changed in monumental ways. I had a baby of my own and spent my days with a bunch of five-year-olds.

With an exhale, I turned off my thoughts about the man behind me and focused on the task at hand. What else did I need? Other than my normal groceries, I planned to grab a few things for tonight. My friend Tina was coming over for a girls' night, and I wanted to have all of our favorite snacks. Chips and salsa, cheese and crackers... Oh. Ice cream!

I snagged a jar of the salsa I liked off the shelf and scanned the chips, searching for my favorite. When I found a row of them on the top shelf, I stepped forward and popped up on my tiptoes. At almost five-seven, I could reach most things, but sometimes I still needed to stretch.

"Jesus," Jay grumbled, suddenly at my back and reaching over my head to grab the bag of tortilla chips.

I bit back a frustrated sigh. What was his issue now?

The heat from his body radiated against mine as I tilted my head back to look up at him. He froze, standing far too close, and stared down at me, his dark brown eyes burning into me. I ran my tongue along my bottom lip, suddenly parched. The way he zeroed in on my mouth made my breath hitch.

"Here." He slowly lowered his arm, tortilla chips in hand and his gaze still locked on me.

I looked away. He didn't need a thirtysomething single mom drooling over him. Images of his bare chest and the basketball shorts hanging low on his hips from the other night flashed through my mind for what had to be the hundredth time.

"Thanks."

As I took the bag from him, Nora grabbed a handful of my hair and yanked, making me flinch.

"Gentle," he coaxed, slowly prying her hand from my hair. His fingers lingered for a moment before he combed through my long locks.

At the sensation, and as his masculine scent enveloped me, heat pooled low in my belly. Being near this man was doing stupid things to my body. I needed to get a grip.

Finally, he blinked several times and stepped back.

Once the heat of him was no longer palpable, I let out a long breath.

The next fifteen minutes moved in slow-motion as I worked to keep my mind focused on my list. It was a challenge, because now I was acutely aware of his presence. I could feel his eyes on me. And the way he fussed over my daughter when she whined or pointed to an object that caught her eye and babbled was so damn distracting.

"Thanks for your help." I put the carton of ice cream in my cart, then turned and held my arms out to take my daughter from him. It took every ounce of willpower I had to ignore the way his T-shirt clung to his biceps and the muscles across his chest.

"It's fine. I can carry her to the checkout lane." He nodded toward the front of the store.

My stomach flipped. I really wanted to get away from him and stop the weird feeling that kept plaguing me. But I resigned myself to spending another ten minutes with him. After all, it would be easier to check out without Nora causing a scene.

After I'd paid, he headed for the door with my daughter,

clearly unwilling to allow me to escape him, then loaded the groceries into the back while I buckled Nora into her car seat.

"Thank you," I said as I stepped back, keeping the back door open.

"No problem." He nodded to the back seat, where Nora was starting to whine. "Is she going to cry the whole way home?"

I sighed. God, I hoped not. "Maybe, but she might fall asleep."

He shook his head, his brows pulling together. "I don't know how you do it."

A dark chuckle escaped me. "It's not like I have a choice."

"Right. I know. I just meant..." He rubbed a hand along his jaw, grimacing.

"It's temporary. That's what I keep reminding myself. It won't last forever."

"If you say so." He shrugged. "Drive safe. Try not to burn the apartment complex down tonight," he said with a smirk as he closed the trunk.

I rolled my eyes, hoping he didn't notice the heat creeping up my neck. "Luckily, my neighbor is a firefighter."

With a chuckle, he waved and headed back toward the store.

As I backed my car out of the parking spot, I couldn't help but watch him retreat. While I shopped, he had followed me and carried Nora, deserting his cart at some point. I couldn't remember if he had much in it when he offered to help. Did he still need to do his own shopping?

And if he did, I didn't know what to make of it. My first impression of him was that he was a jerk, but how many other people in my life would have stopped what they were doing to help me out like that? How many would even bother to ask? Though I supposed I was partly to blame there, since I wasn't good about asking.

Tina was one of a few people in my life who could sense when I needed help. She rarely questioned me, but she'd jump in here and there, always when I was floundering the most. That was likely why she was coming over tonight. I thought I'd done well donning a brave face since I was given the news of the parenting time being approved a couple of days ago. But if the way Tina insisted on coming over tonight and wouldn't take no for an answer, I wasn't sure I was faking it well.

Though I wouldn't argue. The truth was, I could use the distraction.

Later that night, when Tina came back into the living room with a smile on her face, my shoulders sagged with relief. It hit me then that I really needed the break.

"I don't know how you do that." I shook my head.

"Sometimes babies go down for other people better than they do for Mom."

That was probably true. My mom had no problem getting Nora down for naps on the days she watched her. But when we were home, Nora wanted nothing to do with sleep unless I was holding her.

I brought my wineglass to my mouth and sipped it slowly as I surveyed the darkening sky through the sliding glass door.

"You still nervous about Drew getting parenting time?" Tina asked as she sat next to me on the sofa with her own glass.

I shifted and curled my legs under me. "Wouldn't you be?"

"I try not to stress about things I can't do anything about." Her shoulders lifted and fell in a slight shrug. "Have faith in the social worker and probation officer. They'll watch out for Nora. It might feel scary, but it'll all be okay."

I nodded, though anxiety pressed down on my chest like a heavy weight. "I trust that they'll keep her safe, but what if there comes a point when he's allowed unsupervised parenting time? I'm not sure I can handle that."

"We'll cross that bridge when we get there." She patted my knee.

I smiled. There was something comforting about her. She was so motherly. Tina and my own mother were the people I most looked up to. They were women I strived every day to be more like. More than anything, I wanted to be a good mom. The kind Nora deserved. Had I always gotten it right? Nope, definitely not. My mom and Tina had both told me numerous times that I'd make mistakes. Everyone did. All I could do was my best. So I just kept trying. But most days, I still wasn't convinced it was enough.

"Are you ready for the big change this week?" It was time for a different subject so maybe I could turn off all these spiraling thoughts.

She shrugged. "Not much will really change. I actually can't remember the last time Kyle slept at his parents' guest house."

I couldn't either. Kyle practically lived there already, so him officially moving in probably wasn't that big of a deal. Their story gave me hope. Tina had been through so much. She'd lost her husband to war and had been raising two kids on her own before she met Kyle. If she could find love again, then maybe I could too.

My shoulders dropped. For me, I'd yet to find it at all.

All I'd known so far was manipulation, abuse, or indifference when it came to the opposite sex. Here and there, I'd dated a few decent guys, but none had been right for me. Or, more accurately, I hadn't been right for them.

As I studied my friend, taking in her genuine smile, it was obvious Kyle and Tina were made for each other.

For now, I wouldn't give up hope that the person made for me was still out there somewhere.

Chapter Five

JAY

W‌HAT THE HELL? I stomped to my front door, threw it open, and trudged down the hall. Was I losing my damn mind? 'Cause it sure felt like it.

After our run-in at the store last night, things were fairly quiet all evening and into the night. At least until the sun was starting to rise. The early wake-up didn't bother me since I was meeting my sister Izzy for breakfast before my shift.

But now we were back to crying endlessly. Dammit. After a

long shift today, I just wanted to watch the football game in peace.

I banged on her door, though Nora was screaming so loudly I wasn't sure Sarah could hear me. While I waited, I sniffed the air to make sure she wasn't burning food again. The baby quieted, and a moment later the door swung open.

Sarah's eyes widened for an instant, then quickly narrowed on me, her lips turning down.

I hadn't actually considered what I would say or do once I got here, and I was speechless as her green eyes held me captive.

Her hair was pulled up into a messy bun, and her face was makeup free. The look was so different from what I'd seen of her thus far. But even without the perfectly curled hair and makeup, she was gorgeous.

"Yes?" She cocked her hip to the side and lifted Nora higher in her arm.

I sighed, taking a moment to shake myself from my stupor and collect my thoughts.

Nora reached out, opening and closing her little hands, and I swore she said *up*.

"Here. I'll take her." The words spilled out of my mouth without my consent.

"What?" Sarah tilted her head to one side.

"I can hold her while you finish whatever you're doing."

She shook her head. "That's not—"

Nora bounced, cutting off Sarah's words, and leaned toward me, arms still up.

Sarah reluctantly passed her to me, then crossed her arms over her chest.

"I just want to help." I shrugged.

She cocked one eyebrow like she wasn't buying my lame excuse. I didn't blame her.

"And maybe watch the football game in peace."

With a roll of her eyes, she spun on her heel and headed back into the apartment. "Panthers are losing." She nodded to the corner of the living room where her small TV sat, the game already on.

She liked football? Maybe this wouldn't be so bad after all. I could keep Nora quiet and watch the game. Two birds, one stone.

"Mind if I sit down." I gestured to the sofa.

"I was just finishing cleaning the kitchen. I'll only be another ten minutes or so, but sure." She nodded. "Make yourself at home."

I took in her space, surprised by how tidy and simple it all was. I'd assumed that since she had a baby, there would be stuff everywhere. But other than the crib thing, there was no evidence of a baby. Maybe it was because she had so little at all. A sofa with two throw pillows, the small wicker coffee table, and the entertainment stand were all the furniture that made up her living room. She didn't even have a table in the space meant for a dining room. Instead, it was outfitted with a desk and chair.

But in fairness, I'd had no intention of purchasing a dining table for my apartment either. I was a single guy, so why the hell did I need a big-ass dining room table? But my mom had argued with me over it and won, like she always did. Though the only thing it had been good for up until this point was holding all my crap.

Shaking myself out of my thoughts, I made my way over to the sofa and sat down. Nora stretched her legs out, balancing on my left thigh as she bounced and babbled. How did she have so much energy? Especially since she'd been crying on and off for the last hour.

As she continued to bounce, she occasionally bopped my nose. This went on for a solid ten minutes before she relaxed and laid her head on my shoulder and popped her thumb into her mouth.

About that time, Sarah stepped up next to the sofa and peered over, taking in Nora's serene expression. "Do you mind if I put a load of laundry in real quick?"

"Go for it. We're fine."

She eyed me for a moment, wariness and confusion flashing in her eyes, but with a shake of her head, she padded to the back of the apartment.

I relaxed into the cushions, and Nora shifted, burrowing deeper into my chest and neck.

This wasn't bad. Her warm weight was comforting, and she was quiet, which meant I could enjoy the game. Or maybe I could rest my eyes and listen to the game. I should take advantage of the opportunity. Who knew how the night would go once I had to go back to my apartment. Would she stay quiet like this? Her track record said probably not.

I laid my head back and let my eyes drift shut, listening to the announcers. They weren't telling me anything I didn't already know. We were definitely playing like shit.

"Jay," a familiar voice called.

At the sound, I slowly opened my eyes, taking in the way her messy curls rested over large, round tits that strained against a tight white shirt.

I licked my lips, but when she cleared her throat, I tore my gaze away from her chest and back to her face. When had she pulled her hair out of the bun?

"Huh?" I mumbled, my voice hoarse from sleep.

"You fell asleep." She cocked her head to one side. "I'm not sure I really want to risk waking her, but I should try to get her down in her crib."

"Okay." I stood, gently shifting Nora from my hold until a whimper had me freezing. "Will she go back to sleep?"

"If she actually wakes up, probably not." Her lips turned down. Lips that now seemed to have a coat of shine to them that wasn't there earlier. "At least not right away."

"Do you want me to try to put her down?" I had no idea whether that would actually help, but I didn't mind trying.

After a moment, she nodded. "Yeah, maybe. She seems to go down easier for anyone else."

"You might have to walk me through it." I smiled, giving her my best boyish grin.

She chuckled. "A little out of your element?"

In more ways than one, it seemed, since I was struggling to not stare at her glistening lips.

"Yeah, but I'm a quick learner."

She rolled her eyes and headed toward the hallway. I followed, watching her ass sway the whole way.

I carefully placed Nora in the crib and slid my hands out from under her slowly, as Sarah had explained. Surprisingly, she barely stirred. I lingered only for a moment, hypnotized by the way the moonlight was shining through the window, illuminating Sarah's face in the darkened room.

As silently as possible, we crept out into the hall, and once she pulled the door shut behind us, I let out a breath I hadn't realized I was holding. Standing here in the narrow hallway, so close to her, I was tempted to lean forward and find out whether the lip gloss she was wearing was flavored.

I was still considering when she cleared her throat and ducked her head. I wasn't sure what had gotten into me, but I forced my feet to move back through her apartment.

With a small smile that hit me straight in the gut, she held the door open for me. "Thank you."

I nodded and shifted on my feet. "You're welcome."

Tension hung in the air as we stood there awkwardly. It was looking like I had a nice, quiet night in my future. So why I was almost disappointed when she let the door swing shut a moment later?

Although I was grateful that there was no more crying for the rest of the night, I tossed and turned in bed, and images of the green-eyed goddess, with long blond curls and a smile that I wanted to see more of, haunted me throughout the night.

Chapter Six

SARAH

I ADJUSTED the strap of the diaper bag on my shoulder while juggling Nora in the opposite arm as I left my apartment. For once, we weren't running late, but if I didn't get a move on and get her dropped off at my mom's, that would quickly change.

"I must have the magic touch."

Heart thumping against my ribcage, I spun, coming face to face with Jay, whose apartment door swung shut behind him. Jesus, that shit-eating grin of his was making me crazy. It screamed young and cocky. But it needed to come with a warning label: *Will disintegrate panties.*

"Huh?" I shook my head, well aware that I was now staring.

"Nora didn't cry at all after I left."

I fought an eye roll. Of course he thought he was the reason.

"When she fussed, I brought her to bed with me." For weeks, I'd been working to get her to sleep in her crib, but I didn't want Jay back at my door, and frankly, I had been too tired to fight her.

Brows furrowed, he tilted his head in confusion.

With a sigh, I shifted Nora again. "I've been trying to break her of the habit."

"Why?"

Because I wanted my own space back. Because I didn't want to have to be tied to my bed when it was time to put her down. I worried I was messing her up by continuing to encourage the habit that everyone seemed to have an opinion about.

There was no way I would unload all that on this virtual stranger, so I shrugged. "It's better for her."

"Doesn't seem like it. She's probably sad."

I deflated. Great. Yet another person who wanted to put in his two cents. Nora's doctor frowned at the idea. My mom encouraged me to break the habit. Not surprisingly, Tina told me to do what felt right. Now this guy thought I was making my daughter sad. Could I just tell everyone to shut up?

"What about that thing that attaches to the bed?"

I bit back a chuckle. It would have been a great idea nine months ago or so. But Nora just turned one, and it wouldn't be long before she would need an actual bed. So transitioning to a bedside crib just to transition again probably wasn't wise. And honestly, she was already pulling herself up to standing, so it probably wasn't the safest solution either. But now I was curious about how my young, clueless neighbor even knew what a bedside crib was.

"How do you know about those?"

"Oh." He chuckled. "My friend Owen. His girlfriend is pregnant. He was telling me about it. Cece wants to put one on their registry." He cracked that smile of his again. "He worries about how they'll have sex, though."

"Well, I don't have to worry about that," I blurted out.

His eyes widened a fraction, and he gave me a once-over.

My cheeks heated. Why the hell did I say that? It was obvious the thirty-one-year-old single woman with a baby wasn't having sex, but was it really necessary to spell it out for him?

"Gotta get to work." I turned and headed down the hall.

Falling into step beside me, he asked, "What do you do again?"

"I'm a kindergarten assistant."

He waved at an older lady as we moved past her on the sidewalk. "Our new paramedic's girlfriend works at a school too."

"Tina," I said, shifting the diaper bag on my arm again. "She's the teacher I assist."

"Yeah, that's it." He snapped his fingers.

Nora babbled away, pointing at cars and trees as we crossed the parking lot, then waving at Jay and giving him a gummy smile.

"Did she just say *bye*?"

I nodded. Or something close to it, at least. She had gotten really great at repeating sounds.

"Yeah, she's got a few regular words and has been adding to her arsenal pretty often lately. *Up*, *bye* and *Mama* are her favorites, and yesterday, I'm pretty sure she told me *no*."

"She's cute."

I side-eyed him. Until this point, he had seemed more annoyed by her than anything.

"When she's not crying." He sent me that smile again.

My stomach fluttered, but I pushed the feeling away. Though I had to admit the two of them asleep on the sofa last night might have been the most adorable thing I'd ever seen. Even if it made me sad. My daughter would likely never have a close bond with a father figure. So far, I didn't have a good track record when it came to men, not to mention I had doubts that I could truly trust a partner again. Maybe I'd try if it was just me, but now I had to consider Nora and make sure that any people I brought around her would cherish and protect her. Never hurt her.

"Thanks again for last night," I said as I approached my car.

He nodded. "No problem." He studied me for a moment, pursing his lips like maybe he wanted to say more. Instead, he tipped his head and turned, heading across the parking lot.

I tracked him as he sauntered away, my focus drifting lower, locking on to his perfectly toned ass.

I shook my head.

Jesus, I really needed to get a grip.

Chapter Seven

SARAH

I SWALLOWED down my anxiety but refused to make eye contact with Drew as he got out of his car across the street. I'd arrived early in hopes of not having to come face to face with him, yet here he was.

Dammit.

Quickly, I turned and walked down the street to the coffee shop.

How did people do this regularly?

Leaving my baby girl with a social worker and a probation

officer just so her father could have thirty minutes of parenting time with his daughter left me a jittery ball of nerves. I let out a shaky breath and kept my attention fixed on the sidewalk in front of me. I wouldn't turn around and give him the satisfaction of seeing the worry on my face.

I was already a shaky mess, so the last thing I needed was coffee. But I didn't want to be far from Nora, and the coffee shop was close by. I opted for decaf, and when the barista handed me my coffee, I spun, ready to find a quiet corner to sit and stress for the next thirty minutes. As I turned, I almost crashed into a wall of muscle clad in a heather-gray T-shirt and navy-blue suspenders. Stumbling back, I righted myself and got a good look at the man in front of me. Damn. I ran my tongue along my lower lip. I'd never in my life thought I'd find suspenders sexy, but right now, with the way they contrasted with Jay's skintight T-shirt, I did.

Shaking my head, I forced my gaze off his muscular chest and up to his face. But the second I did, I regretted the move. That smile made stupid things happen in my stomach again.

"Whoa. You, okay?"

My shoulders felt strangely warm, and for the first time, I realized he was gripping them.

"Where's Nora?" He swiveled his head, searching the small café.

My chest tightened. "With her father."

His brows pulled together, and a moment later, he released his hold on me and stepped back. "Oh."

I swallowed past the lump in my throat, racking my brain for a way to get out of here without having to tell him that I was killing time while my abusive ex had supervised parenting time with Nora.

It wasn't that cold out. Maybe I'd take my time walking back rather than sitting in the shop.

"See you around, Jay." I tried to mask any sadness in my

voice. Not sure I did so, though.

The need to get out of here was intense. Because I kinda liked this guy. Before Nora, I would have been falling all over this hot, young firefighter, hoping for his attention. It didn't take a brain surgeon to figure out the attraction was mutual. But I had to be better, smarter, than the Sarah I used to be. A night living out the fantasies that wouldn't leave my mind might sound tempting, but it wasn't what I needed anymore. I wanted the kind of connection that would last a lifetime. Not just for me, but for my baby girl. The road I'd traveled so far had been long and full of bumps, but along the journey, I was learning that I deserved more. I could offer more than what my body said I could. And I was done settling for less. I wanted more.

And there was no way a guy in his twenties would want the types of string he'd be stuck with once he discovered the baggage I was carrying.

Jay

EVERY DAY, I was more curious about her story. I guess I'd thought that Nora's dad was no longer in the picture, but the moment she brought him up, Sarah was ready to hightail it out of the café. It was obvious she didn't want to expand on the topic.

I snagged my mobile order from the counter and took off after her. I had no fucking clue what I was doing. Chasing women had never been my thing. But something about this one kept drawing me in.

Once I was at her side, I slowed my pace to match hers. For some unknown reason, she was moving at an excruciating crawl.

Her gaze landed on the big white bag in my one hand before swiveling over to the large drink carrier in my other. "That's a lot of coffee."

"Yeah. I'm on shift today, so I'm picking up coffee and pastries for the guys."

"How nice of you."

I shrugged. "Yeah, I don't mind."

Coffee and abundance of sugar were always met with smiles. The treats were much needed after rough calls. Getting out of the firehouse and enjoying a few minutes of silence was good for me too. Being the fun-loving shit-stirrer of the group meant no one left me alone. But that was a role I'd played my whole life. I liked making people smile and laugh. Even as a kid, my favorite pastime had been entertaining my sisters with jokes or funny faces.

Life was too short to be serious all the time. It was probably why the guys had been giving me a hard time lately. I'd lost a bit of my humor. Apparently, I needed a full eight hours of sleep to be funny.

Sarah checked her phone for the third time since we'd left the coffee shop two minutes ago.

Was she meeting someone? The thought landed like a rock in my gut.

If Nora was with her father, then it wasn't out of the realm of possibility that Sarah would have a date. But it didn't mean I had to like the idea.

"You okay?" The slow pace and the nervous way she kept looking at her phone made it clear that something was up.

"Yeah, I'm just—" She pulled up short beside me.

I stopped too, turning and studying her, then our surroundings. The firehouse was still a half a block up, and the town's diner was coming up on our right. I scanned the street, looking for a person she could be meeting, then focused on Sarah again.

Her body language was different. She looked spooked. Like she was ready to bolt. It was similar to the way she'd behaved the night I met her. Her eyes were wide and full of fear as she stared at a man coming out of the diner. He looked vaguely familiar, but I couldn't place him. I'd been a firefighter in Half Moon Lake for the last three years, but grown up a town over, so I was still getting to know the locals here.

"Everything okay?"

She gave a slight shake of her head. So subtle I almost missed it.

The guy on the sidewalk narrowed his eyes in our direction, the reaction instantly putting me on edge. I shifted forward, the urge to step in front of her, to protect her, swamping me. Sarah remained frozen as he crossed the street to his car. When he approached it, he stood at the driver's side door, staring at us.

Fuck. My stomach was in knots as the interaction played out. When Sarah let out a deep breath like she'd been holding it, I couldn't take it anymore.

"Who's the dude with the greased back hair?" Had no one told him that looked died in the '90s?

"Drew." She unstuck her feet from the sidewalk and moved woodenly toward the entrance to the diner. "Nora's father."

Those two words were like a punch to the gut. The knock-off Danny Zuko? Was she serious? And where was Nora?

Hands fisted at my sides, I hustled to catch up to her again. "Should I be keeping an eye out for this guy?"

I had no problem telling him to take a hike if she didn't want him around.

"No. It's fine." She lowered her head and focused on the concrete in front of her, refusing to meet my gaze. "Thanks for walking with me. I need to go get Nora from the social worker now."

Social worker?

The greaser across the street continued to watch her as we reached the diner's single door. I stepped into his line of vision, making sure he saw me, and finally, he got into his car and drove off.

I hesitated as she disappeared inside. Should I wait here? Before I could make up my mind, the alarms at the firehouse went off, and the decision was made for me. With a heavy rock in my gut, I huffed and jogged back quickly.

Two hours later, I was still thinking about Sarah and Nora, and after the call I'd just gone on, I was even more concerned.

With the trucks put away and ready for our next call, the guys all sat around the large circular table, talking shit and devouring the pastries I'd brought back from the coffee shop this morning.

I pulled out an empty chair, turning it around and straddling it, lost in thought.

"Great job today, Mitchell." The chief patted my shoulder as he walked past us.

"Thanks, Chief."

It had been a team effort. We'd worked quickly and efficiently to extract the mom and baby girl from the car. Luckily, both came out of the accident with nothing more than a few minor scrapes.

Even so, the event had me thinking about another mom and baby that I couldn't seem to get out of my mind.

Chapter Eight

SARAH

THIS WAS why the doctor and my mom had been suggesting I encourage Nora to be a bit more independent. I shifted her in my left arm again, keeping myself between her and the stove-top, and added the vegetables to the pan. It had taken me an hour to get to this stage because Nora wouldn't let me put her down while I made dinner. At this point, I'd be lucky if I ate before nine o'clock.

Letting her sleep in my bed again for the last few nights hadn't helped the separation anxiety. That was for sure. But it had been just as much for me as it was for her. It was harder for me to let her fuss after Drew's visit with her earlier this week. But we were starting over tonight because I really needed her to learn to self soothe. I was only one person, and it was unrealistic for me to hold her all the time.

With a renewed determination, I headed back into the living room where her Pack 'n' Play was set up. She clung to me as I set her down and put a few toys in front of her. And, of course, within a minute, she was screaming at the top of her lungs.

Be strong, I chanted silently as I forced myself back into the kitchen.

Just as I was stirring the veggies, a loud banging from the front door startled me, making me jump.

Though my heart was racing, I couldn't help but smile. Jay was the only one who ever showed up unannounced.

Shaking my head, I scolded myself. Nope. Not going there.

The warm smile that greeted me when I pulled the door open was harder to ignore than the scowl he'd sported last time he'd appeared like this.

He stepped inside. "Can I help?"

Despite the butterflies erupting in my stomach, my heart sank. I still wasn't sure what his motivations were. But regardless, having someone else hold her wasn't the solution either.

I shook my head. "You don't have to."

"I know. But she's been crying on and off for the last two hours." He sniffed the air. "We both know what happened the last time you were cooking and got distracted by her."

I rolled my eyes. Jeez. I burned food *one* time, but apparently, I'd never live it down.

But I was hungry, so if he wanted to sit with Nora so I could finish dinner, then I should just accept the help.

"Would you mind just sitting on the floor with her while

she plays with toys?" I scooped Nora out of her Pack 'n' Play. "I don't want her falling asleep this early."

He tilted his head to the side. "Can I put the game on again?"

"Sure." Being a football fan myself, I would never mind watching a game. Usually, I had one on in the background while I was cleaning or cooking.

After getting Nora situated on the rug with a few toys, I left her with Jay and went back into the kitchen to finish my stir-fry.

"That smells really good," Jay called from his spot on the floor.

I turned and smiled at the scene. He was holding up a rattle doll in front of Nora, making it dance. Nora's giggles were the best thing I'd heard all night.

"Would you like some?" The least I could do was offer the guy a plate of food.

"Uh, sure." He shrugged. "Was just gonna order a pizza again, but this smells too good to pass up."

"Do you not cook?"

He shook his head. "Nah. I make a mean PB&J and can cook ramen or throw a frozen pizza in the oven." His attention was still focused on Nora, but his words were directed at me. "But I lived at home until a few weeks ago. My mom did most of the cooking."

The spoon I was holding clattered to the countertop. I knew he was young, but wow.

I hadn't lived at home for almost ten years now.

He finally looked up, meeting my gaze, and gave me a sheepish shrug. "I can throw simple things together, but no, I don't really cook."

This dinner wasn't anything special, but I made a pretty decent stir-fry. The trick was not to overcook the vegetables. That way they still had a bit of a crunch to them. But suddenly,

I felt self-conscious. I rarely cooked for other people. Heck, I didn't even have a dining room table. Now, I wished I had. We'd have to sit on the sofa or floor in the living room or on the other side of the island that served as a breakfast counter. At least I'd had the good sense to buy a few stools when I'd moved in last year. Though that good sense had clearly left. Otherwise, I would be telling Jay to go back to his apartment.

But I wanted him to stay. Having a meal and adult conversation sounded pretty perfect right about now.

Chapter Nine

JAY

Sarah stepped into the living room, wringing her hands like she was nervous.

"Food is ready. Sorry I don't have a table for us to sit at." She waved to the island. "It's usually just me, so I don't really need a table." With a shrug, she frowned.

"This is fine." I patted the floor beside me.

Her eyes widened as she studied me. I wasn't sure what surprised her. I couldn't count how many times I'd sat on the floor with my sisters and our PB&Js watching TV. That was how our evenings always went when our mom had to work late. Dad was a firefighter, so he worked odd hours, including evenings and overnights.

"That way we can sit with Nora." I tickled the little girl's belly when I said her name.

The giggle that erupted from her made my chest warm and a smile stretch across my face.

"I'm assuming that if we put her back in that thing," I said, waving at the baby jail against the wall, "she'll cry."

Sarah rolled her eyes. "It's a Pack 'n' Play. Plenty of people use them, and their babies have no issues. It's definitely just a Nora thing."

She turned and grabbed the bowls from the counter. "Do you want something to drink?"

"Water is fine."

As she approached and set the bowls on the coffee table, her movements were still tremulous, but when she reappeared a few moments later with two glasses of water, she seemed more at ease.

"He should have thrown it." She shook her head as she sat down with her bowl in her hands.

"Huh?"

"Moore." She tipped her head toward the TV. "He holds on to the ball too long. Then he gets sacked or tries to run it to gain a yard or two. They really need a new quarterback after this season."

I turned my attention back to the TV just as the announcers were chiming in with the same sentiment. I missed the sack because the gorgeous blonde sitting a few feet away had captured my attention. It happened more and more every time I was around her.

I was impressed by her football knowledge. It was honestly the only sport I consistently followed.

"Yeah," I said. "I had him on my fantasy football roster at

the beginning of the season but took him off a couple of weeks ago because he's been freezing in the pocket." I brought the fork to my mouth and took a bite. The mix of sweet and spicy was perfection.

"I wish I could keep up with mine."

"Yours?" I raised an eyebrow at her.

"Yeah. I have good intentions every year, but by this point in the season, it's usually a lost cause. My dad nags me about it, so you would think I wouldn't forget."

I was intrigued. "Do you create a team just to appease your dad?"

"My dad is a huge football fanatic, so fantasy league and watching games together is our thing." Her shoulders rose and fell as she took another bite of her food. "I was cheerleading captain in high school. Between that and my dad, I know a pretty good amount. I love the idea behind fantasy football, and I'm excited at the beginning of every season. But I don't know. Life happens, and I get sidetracked easily, I guess. Especially now that I have Nora."

Her phone chimed from where it sat on the floor next to her, pulling her attention away from me. She unlocked the screen, and her eyes went wide in the same way they had earlier today outside the diner. Just as quickly as the expression appeared, though, it was gone again.

"What is it?" I asked, chills running down my spine.

She shook her head and placed her phone face down on the carpet. "Just a wrong number."

My stomach twisted at the fear that clashed across her face, but I'd let it go for now. We were neighbors, and I was helping her out. It wasn't like I could demand she open up and tell me what was going on. But I had this weird need to get to know her more, and I wanted her to trust me. To feel comfortable letting her guard down.

I guess I just had to earn it.

Chapter Ten

SARAH

As I SET the last grocery bag on the counter, I looked around. Somehow, I'd subconsciously picked up enough to make dinners for two.

Jay had been over all but two nights this past week. I assumed he was on shift when he wasn't with us.

But when he was here, we would fall into an easy routine. I'd start dinner, then Nora would fuss. Within a few minutes, Jay would show up at my door and keep her occupied while I cooked. Then we would eat and watch football or a show on

Netflix. We both liked comedies, so choosing what to watch was never an issue.

Nora, miraculously, was playing nicely in her Pack 'n' Play while I put the groceries away. I hated to admit it, but it was almost disappointing that she wasn't fussing. If she didn't cry, then I couldn't expect Jay to show up at my door.

A high-pitched squeal of delight pulled my attention. Nora was bouncing and pushing the buttons on the stuffed elephant, making it light up and say the phrases it had been programmed to make.

A knock sounded on the door a moment later, and for a fleeting moment, I hoped it was Jay. But that was unlikely since Nora wasn't crying.

Yet it was Jay who appeared when I swung the door open.

One brow raised, he tilted to one side and peered around me. "Thought I heard her crying."

Does he just sit outside my door waiting for Nora to make the slightest sound?

"Oh." Although I desperately wanted him to come in, I wasn't going to lie. "Nah, she was just squealing over a new toy my mom got her."

Nodding, he shuffled his feet and sent me that smile of his that I *really* needed to stop obsessing over.

"Well, I'm here now anyway. I can sit with her..."

"Oh." I clasped my hands in front of me and looked from him to Nora and back again. "You don't need to."

"I know. But—I want to." The last of his words were laced with so much sincerity.

My heart panged and my throat went tight. "Are you sure?"

In response, he stepped inside, coming so close I had no choice but to back up and pull the door open wider.

He swung Nora up into his arms, and she proceeded to bop him on the nose. With a chuckle at the two of them, I made my way back into the kitchen. He was so good with her, or at least he had come a long way from that day in the grocery store.

"Did you update your lineup yet?"

I didn't even realize he had stepped into the kitchen behind me until he spoke. He held Nora in one arm and was unloading groceries and placing them on the island with the rest.

I sighed as I grabbed the milk and turned to the fridge. "On top of being hounded by my dad, I've got you reminding me too?"

He chuckled. "I offered to do it for you."

There were moments when I regretted giving him my phone number. But mostly, I'd enjoyed the few texts we'd shared about fantasy football and who I should update my roster with.

"I updated it during lunch today."

As we continued to put the groceries away and I preheated the oven, we chatted about tonight's game and made guesses about who would win.

My phone vibrated on the kitchen island, interrupting the conversation. As I held it up and read the message, I let out a huff. This was starting to get annoying. At least it wasn't Drew texting me. That was my fear when the first message had come through last week. But it was obvious it was a wrong number. Or scammers.

"Everything okay?"

I glanced over at Jay, who was leaning back against the island, Nora still nestled in one arm, his brows now furrowed.

"Yeah, just random texts from a strange number."

"Same one as the other night?"

I nodded. "But it's weird things. Like this one. *Good running into you at the gas station.* I didn't even get gas today."

"Hmm. Have you messaged back and let them know they're texting the wrong number?"

"No." I shook my head. "My dad was telling me a few

months ago about wrong number text scams. I bet that's what this is, and you aren't supposed to text them back."

He stared at me for a long moment, his jaw working like he wanted to say something else, but a moment later, he straightened and wandered over to turn the TV on while I turned back to preparing dinner.

I tried a new recipe tonight, one that I'd seen on Instagram, and I was pretty sure it was a hit, since Jay asked for seconds.

"Meatball sliders are my new favorite thing." He wiped his mouth with his napkin. "Can you teach me how to make these? The guys at the house would love 'em."

I raised an eyebrow at him. "I thought you didn't cook."

He shrugged. "I don't. But I think I could learn." That smirk of his curled his lips. "You know, with the right teacher." He shot me a wink.

My stomach fluttered. God, I was being ridiculous. How the hell did one wink from this guy cause such a reaction? Was I that deprived of male attention?

Yeah, I absolutely was, but when my gaze locked onto his again, the smirk was gone. He was laser focused on my mouth, and I swore the attraction wasn't one-sided.

I ran my tongue along my bottom lip. Jay tracked the movement, and maybe it was my imagination, but I was pretty sure he let out a subtle groan.

Excitement coursed through me and butterflies took flight in my belly. Was he going to kiss me?

His phone rang loudly from the coffee table, startling us both and breaking the spell we'd fallen under.

Glancing at it, he said, "Sorry, I have to take this. It's my sister."

He had talked about the younger one a bit over the last week. She attended the University of North Carolina in Asheville, commuting from their parents' house.

He hung up and sent me a sad smile. "Sorry, I have to go. Izzy needs a ride home from a party."

I nodded. From our conversations, I'd gathered that his sisters depended on him a lot. I was an only child, so I couldn't really relate, but it was super sweet that he made them a priority and was sure to be available when they needed him.

But a few minutes later, when I shut the door behind him, sadness and disappointment washed over me.

It was probably for the best that we had been interrupted, though. Nothing good could come from pining over my young next-door neighbor.

Chapter Eleven

JAY

I SIGHED as Izzy rambled on about how shitty her boyfriend was. She had refused to take my advice the last time we'd had a conversation like this, so I wasn't sure what she wanted me to say.

Not wanting to start an argument with her, I kept my mouth shut and let her vent.

When she finally paused to take a breath, I couldn't hold in my opinion any longer. "I've told you a dozen times to get rid of that tool."

She rolled her eyes. "You say that about every guy I date."

"Yep. Because they're all tools." I huffed. "Your *boyfriend* should be the one giving you a ride home, not me."

The asshole had agreed to be the designated driver before they went out. Then he'd gotten wasted and couldn't take her home. Talk about a walking red flag.

Izzy's eyes widened. "What's your deal? You always say I can call you if I need a ride. So why the bitch fest? You could have just said no."

She should know me better than that. I'd never say no to either of my sisters when they asked for help.

I clenched my teeth and pushed away my annoyance. "It's fine."

"Jeez, I should have just ubered."

I laughed at the ridiculousness of that. "Getting an Uber out here at ten p.m. would have been impossible." Small towns in the middle of nowhere didn't have reliable rideshares.

She shrugged. "If you were busy, I would have figured it out."

"I wasn't busy. I was just hanging out—"

I snapped my mouth shut. What could I say? I was hanging out with the single mom who lived next door to me? Izzy would have a field day with that one.

"Wait." Her face lit with a smile, and she did some weird bounce in her seat. "You have a girlfriend, don't you?"

"No." I shook my head, but even as I did, it hit me that maybe that was what I wanted.

I'd hated having to leave Sarah and Nora tonight. Every night, really. Only a few weeks ago, I'd been in a rush to move out and get my own space. But now I had no interest in sitting in my apartment alone. The gorgeous blonde next door was constantly on my mind. I wanted to be near her, and tonight the urge to kiss her had been overwhelming. Ever since I'd left her apartment, it was all I could think about.

"Way to be sus."

I rolled my eyes at my sister's dramatics. I wasn't acting suspicious at all. "She's just my next-door neighbor."

"Next-door neighbor..." She frowned, her brows pulling together. Then she whipped her head toward me and her eyes widened comically. "Bruh, no way. The one with the crying baby?"

A week or so after I moved into the apartment, I'd complained to her about the baby next door that cried all night long.

She laughed. "I'm shook. And Angie is gonna die."

I rubbed a hand down my face. "Don't you dare. She reads too many romance novels. She'll concoct some elaborate story of how this'll play out."

"She'll totally ship you." She bounced in her seat again. "She's convinced I need to date older men so my story can be an age gap."

With a shake of my head, I gripped the steering wheel a little tighter. I never thought anything would rival the madness that was my sisters as teenagers, yet here we were.

After Izzy and I made plans for breakfast this week, I headed back to my apartment, secretly hoping—and feeling like an asshole because of it—that Nora would be crying when I returned.

She didn't make a peep all night long. Too bad I didn't sleep at all. I was too busy thinking about Sarah's blond curls laid out on my pillow as she moaned my name over and over again.

Chapter Twelve

JAY

SPENDING the evening next door had become a ritual I looked forward to. I was done fighting my attraction to Sarah, and I enjoyed spending time with Nora just as much as I did with her mama.

As a young guy living in a one-bedroom apartment with a job that had crazy hours, I didn't have a lot to offer. But something about her kept pulling at me, and I wasn't one to shy away from going after what I wanted. I'd always lived by the motto that it's better to try and fail than never try at all.

Unfortunately, that plan would have to wait a couple of days. I was working the night shift for the next two nights, but then I'd have two days off.

"You in or not?" Kyle's voice brought my attention back to the game of rummy we were starting.

I nodded.

When I realized that I'd be on shift with Kyle tonight, I was determined to broach the subject of Sarah. Specifically, if he knew anything about these random text messages she'd been getting. My gut was telling me something wasn't right. Scammers didn't typically send texts day after day like she'd been getting over the last week.

"How well do you know Tina's assistant, Sarah?"

Kyle straightened and narrowed his eyes at me. "Why?"

"Just curious how much you know about her." I shrugged.

"Huh, I'd like to ask the same question."

"He's her neighbor," Owen chimed in from his spot next to Kyle.

Beside me, Logan chuckled. I shot a glare his way, then turned back to Owen, who was doing a shit job of covering up his smirk. Both of these assholes had been giving me shit for weeks. At first, they teased me about being so bent out of shape about the baby crying all the time. Over the last week, they'd been razzing me about spending so much platonic time with the beautiful blonde who lived next to me.

"Shut up, ass," I mumbled.

"Wait..." Kyle angled forward and cocked his head to the side. "You're the baby whisperer?"

My heart thudded in my chest. *Did she call me that?*

I couldn't stop the smile that spread across my face.

"Yeah, asshole's already got more experience with babies than me, and I'm the one with one on the way," Owen teased.

"She has enough to deal with. Leave her alone," Kyle grumbled, throwing down a pair of aces.

66

That was the problem, though, wasn't it? She was alone and needed help.

With a shake of my head, I cleared my throat. "She's been getting weird texts. She says they're nothing, but..."

Kyle leaned back in his chair and frowned. "Ask her about her ex. It could be him."

"Drew?"

"Yeah." He nodded. "Ask her what happened when she was pregnant with Nora."

His eyes went hard as he spoke, making it obvious that whatever it was hadn't been good. I opened my mouth to ask what the hell had happened, but he shook his head and cut me off with his next words.

"Not my story to tell. But I could talk to Dylan over at the police department about the texts. Have him look into it."

Dylan Gray had recently been promoted to lieutenant, and from what I understood, he was looking to take the detectives' exam sometime in the next year.

I nodded. Hell yeah. I needed to know she was safe. Nora too.

From there, we dove into our game and the conversation shifted, but my focus stayed on the two blondes who seemed to be always on my mind lately.

Chapter Thirteen

JAY

My APARTMENT DOOR slammed shut behind me a moment before I was knocking on Sarah's door. I didn't even wait for Nora to make a sound. I needed Sarah to know I was here because of her and not just Nora.

When she opened the door wearing a tight red sweater that clung to her large tits, with red painted lips to match, I couldn't stop the groan that slipped out.

We were heading into dangerous territory. I wanted this woman, but I needed her to know that it wasn't just physical. I enjoyed spending time with her, texting about fantasy football, or just laughing at some stupid show we were watching.

"Are you coming in?"

Blinking back to consciousness, I nodded. Guess I couldn't stand here all night staring at her. I stepped forward, and when she tilted her head back to look up at me, I reached out and tucked one of her curls behind her ear. "You look amazing in this sweater."

With that, I brushed past her with a smirk.

She opened her mouth but closed it again and shook her head, moving away from the door.

"Do you like Indian food?"

I scooped Nora up into my arms from where she sat on the floor and turned back toward Sarah. "Love it."

"Perfect. I'm making chicken tikka masala."

"Sounds great. Want to watch a movie tonight or more *Brooklyn Nine-Nine*?"

She tilted her head to the side, her expression thoughtful.

A movie meant more time together, so I was secretly hoping she picked that option.

"A movie sounds good."

Fighting the urge to pump a fist, I moved to the island and set Nora on it with my arms braced on either side. Sarah followed, padding back to the stove. This had also become part of our routine over the last week. I would sit with Nora and talk to Sarah as she made dinner.

Tonight, the topic of conversation was the changes she should make to her fantasy roster before Sunday's game. Her family always counted her out by late October because she stopped checking it. I planned to change that. We were three weeks into November. My hope was that when she went to her family's Thanksgiving next week, she'd arrive with a fresh win in her pocket.

"If I beat my cousin Tim this week, he's going to lose his mind." She looked back at me over her shoulder and smirked.

"Well, then he'll lose his mind. As long as nothing crazy happens this week, you have a good chance." The rest of the night went perfectly, although I spent the entire evening in various degrees of hard. Every time she bent even slightly forward, her large tits in that tight red sweater looked like they were ready to pop out.

I was a mix of relieved and disappointed when she announced that she was going to put Nora down for bed. As much as I needed a moment where I wasn't imagining her full breasts spilling out of that damn sweater, I also wasn't ready for the night to be over.

Once I'd loaded the last of the dishes from dinner, I shut the dishwasher. I'd just started it when Sarah stepped into the kitchen.

She shook her head. "She went right down. Lately, she's been getting better about sleeping in her crib." With her lips pressed together in a small smile, she scanned the kitchen. "You did the dishes?"

I shrugged. "I just loaded the dishwasher. You cooked. I cleaned up. It was the rule in my house growing up. When Mom made dinner, one of us was responsible for cleanup."

She sighed. "You didn't have to."

How many times did I need to tell this woman that *I wanted to*? Maybe it was time I showed her instead. I closed the space between us, and when her eyes widened and she tilted her head back, blinking at me, I couldn't help but smirk. I cupped her cheek with one hand as I trailed the other one down her shoulder and grasped her hip.

"I've thought about kissing you almost every second of the day since we were interrupted the other night."

Her eyes drifted closed, and she hummed a sound of satisfaction. "Me too."

Good. I wanted to satisfy her in other ways, but for now, I needed to finally find out what her lips tasted like.

I brushed the hair from her cheek and ran my fingers through her long curls. Fisting them in my hand, I brought my mouth down on hers. Her warm lips moved against mine as I deepened the kiss, thrusting my tongue inside. I pulled her body flush against mine, knowing full well she could feel the effect a simple kiss was having on me.

When I released her, she stepped back out of my embrace, chest heaving and eyes wide.

My heart thumped in my chest. Was she surprised by the kiss or regretting it?

Questions flitted through her eyes as she brought her fingers up to her slightly swollen lips.

Her phone chimed from the island countertop, and for a moment, she just stared at me. Finally, she let out a breath and picked it up.

The instant she unlocked the screen, her body went stiff, and she gasped.

Stomach sinking, I stepped up behind her, and when I saw the text on the screen, it dropped straight to the floor.

You've always looked good in red.

Maybe I could have let her play this one off as a wrong number if she weren't wearing a bright red sweater.

"This isn't a wrong number." I said over her shoulder. "Is it Drew?"

"What?" She spun around, eyes wider than before, and clasped her phone to her chest.

"Tell me, Sarah." I swallowed past the lump in my throat. "Please tell me what's going on."

Shoulders slumping, she turned and shuffled into the living

room. The moment she sank onto the sofa, I knew I wasn't going to like what she was about to say.

As Sarah recounted the story of how he'd beaten her when she was four months pregnant, landing him an eighteen-month incarceration, my blood pressure skyrocketed. Fuck.

He'd only been released a month ago, apparently for good behavior. I gritted my teeth at that last part.

"Looking back, maybe I should have called the police that night he got me pregnant instead of giving him what he wanted. But it was easier to give in to him when he got angry than it was to stand up for myself. It was the only thing that stopped him from hurting me."

Heart cracking, I cleared my throat. "How long?" I'd probably regret asking for more details, but I needed to know. The more information I had, the better equipped I'd be to protect her.

She dropped her chin, wringing her hands in her lap. "How long were we together?"

I nodded.

"Two years. Things were okay—not great, but not bad either—until a month after we moved in together." She pressed her lips together and inhaled a deep breath before letting it out slowly. "After that first time, when he put bruises around my neck, I learned that it was much easier to be complacent and let him do what he wanted."

My jaw locked tighter. I'd never contemplated murder until that moment.

"After I finally left, I thought I was free." Her voice cracked, and tears crested her lashes. "I filed a restraining order, and when I found out I was pregnant, I thought that as long as I never admitted that the baby was his, it would be fine. But he found out about my pregnancy, and when I wouldn't tell him the truth, it made him the angriest I'd ever seen him."

Her tears came faster then, the sight hitting me like a punch to the gut. I wrapped one arm around her and pulled her into my side. Fuck. For the first time in my adult life, I was at a loss as to what to do. Half of me wanted to sit here and hold her for as long as she needed, and the other half wanted to find Drew and throttle him.

"We should look into who's sending the texts." If it was Drew, we needed to take action. The guy was obviously prone to violence, and these situations almost always escalated.

She nodded against my shoulder. "I talked to my lawyer after the last text, just to be sure. All he could find out is that they are coming from a disposable cell." She lifted her head to look at me, her eyes still shimmering with tears. "He's trying to dig deeper, but without proof that it's Drew, there's nothing we can do."

"I know someone at the police department. I can ask him to look into it too." I didn't mention the conversation Kyle and I had a few days ago. If she got upset about the overstep, I'd take the blame. Sarah didn't have many friends, and Tina seemed to be the closest. There was no way I'd mess that up for her.

She shook her head. "You don't have to—"

I took her face in my hands, forcing her to look at me. "Sarah, please stop telling me I don't have to. I know that. But I *want* to. I want to make sure you and Nora are safe. And happy. I *want* to be here." I swallowed hard as her eyes continued to widen with my words. "Let me do this, please."

Maybe she didn't want me here as much as I wanted to be here. But as she searched my face, she nodded.

Hit with a wave of relief, I pressed my lips to her forehead.

Chapter Fourteen

SARAH

PART of me thought maybe I'd imagined the kiss Jay and I had shared a few nights ago. Until last night, when he kissed me again before leaving my apartment. It was probably my experience with shitty guys over the last ten years, but I assumed the kiss meant he wanted sex. Yet he'd made no move in that direction. I still wasn't sure how I felt about that. As much as I wanted his hands on me, it felt good to just spend time with him. It also made me realized how lonely I'd been over the last year. Nora kept me busy, and she was my sole focus, so it wasn't surprising that I hadn't noticed.

With a sigh, I put the car in park and stared at the front of the diner where I was meeting the social worker for Drew's parenting time. Once I got Nora out of her seat, and as I shut the back door and turned, I jumped.

Jay was standing a few feet away, leaning casually against the front of his black Jeep.

"What are you doing here?" Had I been so engrossed in my thoughts that I didn't see him when I pulled into the parking spot?

"Supporting you. I don't like the idea of you being here alone with Drew around." He pushed off the car and came to stand in front of me.

"The social worker is here." I shrugged, refusing to meet his intense stare. We both knew he could see through my fake bravado. As long as Drew was free, I wouldn't feel safe.

"Don't care." He gently cupped the sides of my face, and instantly, my whole body relaxed.

I tilted my head up to look into his eyes.

"I feel better knowing you and Nora are safe." His gaze turned hard as he looked over my head. "Come on."

He took Nora from me and adjusted her in one arm. She immediately assumed her normal position by snuggling into the crook of his neck. Jay settled his free hand on the small of my back, then guided me down the sidewalk that led to the front door of the diner.

Without turning, I could feel Drew's glare from across the street. My skin felt like it was crawling with bugs as his gaze raked over me. As much as I wanted to ignore him, the fear had me glancing nervously to where he stood by his car.

When our eyes met, he shot me a menacing smirk that made my stomach turn. Why had I ever found him attractive?

"In we go," Jay said, pulling open the door of the diner.

Last time, the handoff had been difficult. Nora had cried, but by the time I was outside and had looked back in, she was better. Today was so much worse. She clung to Jay, and as the social worker gently pried her free, she screamed for me. Even the ice cream she offered her wasn't enough to distract Nora. I was sure Jay was ready to say *screw it, arrest me. We're not doing this.* But just as quickly as his face flashed with anger, it fell in resignation. Like he was remembering that I would be the one who would be held accountable. So, with our heads hung and our hearts aching, we walked away as Nora cried.

"Now I know why you looked so upset the last time you did this." He held open the door for me.

Nora's cries still echoed through the small diner as I stepped out in front of him. Rather than look at Drew again, I forced myself to keep my focus forward as we walked down the sidewalk away from the diner.

"It was the hardest thing I'd ever done, and this time was even harder."

He laced his fingers with mine and gave my hand a squeeze. As much as I hated this whole thing, I had to admit that it was easier with him here. The next half hour went by quickly, even though we were both quiet. But sitting beside Jay, with his arm draped over my shoulders while we drank our coffees, was not only comforting, but it kept my anxiety at bay.

As we made our way back down the street, a group of people gathered outside the diner's entrance caught my attention. The couple with their backs to me looked awfully familiar.

My chest tightened a little. Was that the paramedic who'd come over to Jay's apartment when I burned the chicken that first night? And the cute pregnant blonde with him must be his girlfriend, Cece. Once we got a little closer, I could see the other people were Tina and Kyle.

"What are you guys doing here?" I asked, stopping at the edge of the group.

Tina turned, tilting her head slightly. "Aren't we grabbing dinner?" She looked from Kyle to Jay, wearing a confused frown.

I surveyed Jay, who nodded but was still silent. Suddenly, his face went hard, and movement at the diner's entrance caught my eye.

Drew exited, and Jay followed his every movement with his eyes.

"You don't have to do all this..." I let the last word trail off. Every time I said something like that, he reminded me that he wanted to. And the look he was now giving me said the same thing.

"*Yes*, I do." He pressed a hand to the small of my back. "He needs to know you have people in your life who are looking out for you."

Tina's eyes widened, and she took a step closer to me. "I'm getting a feeling you have some explaining to do."

Stomach sinking, I lowered my head. I didn't want to worry one of my closest friends. "I'll fill you in later."

She narrowed her eyes slightly at me but didn't say anything else.

I kept my focus on the sidewalk in front of me, but it was impossible not to feel Drew's attention as he crossed the street.

When his car door slammed shut and he tore off, Jay put gentle pressure on my back and led me to the front entrance. "Let's go get our girl and eat dinner with friends."

I froze, my feet sticking to the pavement.

Our girl?

Jay looked down at me, and warmth flooded my system. I could see it in his eyes. There was no surprise or regret. He just unapologetically embraced what he'd said.

And the scared, broken girl inside me finally felt hope for the first time in a very long time. But could I trust him? And could I trust myself to believe that this could be something real?

Chapter Fifteen

JAY

HEAD SHAKING and with a smile on my face, I knocked on her door. Nora wasn't crying, but she hadn't been any of the dozen times I'd shown up here over the last two weeks. Hopefully, by now, Sarah understood what I wanted. What my intentions were.

I refused to sit in my apartment alone when I wanted to be here with them. Again, I had to laugh at myself. For months, I'd wanted to be alone and in my own space, and now that I had that, I wanted to be somewhere else entirely.

The routine Sarah and I had gotten into was the best part of my day. I would show up, and she would open the door, that gorgeous knowing smile directed at me.

Except not this time. The moment the door swung open, I could tell something was wrong. The skittish, frazzled woman I had met that first night was back.

"What's wrong?" I followed her into the apartment.

She stood in the middle of the open living room, scanning the space and wringing her hands.

"I don't know." Her voice wavered as she spoke. "I think someone's been in here."

"What?" I snapped.

She spun back to me, fear and uncertainty settling over her like a dark cloud.

I took in a deep breath, wanting to kick myself for using such a rough tone. "Sorry. Didn't mean for that to come out so harshly. But what do you mean you think someone's been in here?"

"Maybe I'm just losing my mind." She shook her head. "But things seem like they've been moved."

Her phone vibrated where it sat on the coffee table. I swear to God I would lose my mind if it was another text from that *wrong* number. We all knew it was that piece of shit wannabe Danny Zuko.

By the time she picked it up and gasped, covering her mouth with her hand, I was at her side.

Shaking, she handed me the phone.

> You look beautiful in that dress today.

What the hell?

I'd had the same thought when she opened the door a second before, but it had evaporated the moment I'd seen her face.

God dammit.

"I'm staying here tonight."

"What? You don't need—"

I placed my finger on her lips. Even terrified, she was affected by my touch. Her eyes went wide, then heated. Damn, did I want to cover her mouth with mine until we both forgot all about the danger that lurked.

"What do I keep telling you?"

She smiled behind my finger.

"I'll say it over and over again if I have to." I brushed a finger along her cheek and tucked a strand of hair behind her ear. "I *want* to. I want to be here and take care of you and Nora. You are important to me, and I need to know you're both safe."

I threaded my fingers through her hair and then rested my hand at the back of her neck. More than anything, I wanted to claim her mouth, but I held back, giving her ample time to pull away. But when her eyes drifted closed and she tilted forward, I met her halfway, molding my lips to hers. This kiss was different from the last few. It was desperate and frenzied. And I wanted so much more.

A loud-pitched giggling pulled me from the moment. We broke apart, and in unison, we turned to look at Nora, who stood holding on to the edge of the coffee table and reaching out for us.

I let go of Sarah, ready to scoop her up.

"Wait," Sarah breathed, her hand landing on my forearm.

Nora giggled again, wobbling in place. Then she was moving. Three quick steps forward before she wobbled once more and plopped down on her butt.

"Oh my god, she did it."

The awe in Sarah's voice made me chuckle. We had talked about this for the last three nights. She was certain that Nora would take her first steps any day, and she was right. I got the excitement. I was feeling the awe too. It was one thing to know it would happen, but another thing entirely to witness it.

"You said she would soon." I scooped Nora off the floor.

She sighed. "I'm so glad I got to see it. I was afraid she'd do it while I was working."

I brought Nora closer to her mama, and Sarah tickled her belly, praising her.

A conversation with my dad a few years ago came to mind as I soaked in the moment. He had told me that when I found the woman that I wanted to spend forever with, I'd just know it. At the time, I had rolled my eyes. He'd been lecturing me because I wasn't ready to bring the girl I was dating home to meet my parents.

But right here, right now, his words made total sense.

Chapter Sixteen

SARAH

TONIGHT FELT WEIRD. Different. And not just because I was freaked out that someone may have been in my apartment. That was probably just me being paranoid. What had changed was the way Jay kept looking at me as I cooked dinner and we ate.

As I stepped into the living room area, I froze. I'd just put Nora down for the night in her crib, and out here, Jay was pulling a throw blanket out of the basket I kept in the corner full of them.

"Are you cold?"

"What?" He turned, his brows furrowed, then looked down at the blanket in his hand and chuckled. "I wasn't kidding when I said I'm staying here." He waved at the sofa. "Saw the basket of blankets and figured I'd get one out for me tonight."

I shook my head. "You don't need—"

"What do I keep telling you?"

I rolled my eyes, even as my heart tripped over itself. "I was going to say you don't need to sleep on the couch. We can share my bed."

His eyes widened instantly. "No we cannot."

Stomach dropping and hopes disintegrating, I crossed my arms across my chest. "Why not?"

Did I smell or—

He took three large steps toward me, closing the space between us, and gripped my hips. As he pulled me tight against his very muscular body, I gasped.

"There's no way I could sleep in bed with you and not touch you." He shifted me so I could feel his hardness through his sweatpants. "See what just talking about being in a bed with you is doing to me?"

I took a brave breath in and hoped to God he wanted the same thing I did. Because I was done pretending that I didn't want him.

"Who says you couldn't touch me?" I slowly trailed both hands up under the hem of his shirt. "Jay, I want you. I want to feel your hands on me."

"Sarah." He searched my face, his eyes so earnest.

I shifted to rub against him, pulling a groan from him.

"I'm not looking for something casual or a one-time thing," he murmured. "When I make you come on my cock, it will be because we're together."

My heart leapt, and I nodded so quickly I felt like a bobble-head. "I want that too. So much."

His gaze darkened to a rich brown a second before his lips crashed down on mine. I ran my fingernails up his back as he devoured my mouth. Snaking both hands around to cup my ass, he lifted me, bunching my dress around my hips. I moaned into his mouth as I wrapped my legs around him, feeling the hard length of his erection pressing against me. He walked backward and dropped down onto the couch. Breathless, I broke the kiss and pulled back, placing my hands on his chest and grinding back and forth against him.

"Fuck," he gritted out. "I can feel how wet you are."

"I need to feel you inside me." I rocked again.

He gripped my hips, stopping me. "Sarah, I don't have anything with me."

I tilted my head to the side, frowning.

"Protection," he spit out like he hated to admit it.

"Oh."

Of course. The last thing most guys would want was to be tied to a woman because of a baby.

I shook my head, stopping the jaded girl inside me from taking over. "I'm on birth control, and I was tested for everything under the sun when I was pregnant. And I haven't... you know... been with anyone since then."

Single moms with babies rarely had guys banging down their doors. Though I supposed the hot firefighter beneath me had literally done just that the night I met him. I smiled at the reminder.

"I'm good too." He tightened his hold and moved my hips back and forth. "I want nothing more than to find out how wet you are."

I took over, loving the look on his face every time I glided over the tip and then back down. We were still clothed, but based on the way his eyes rolled back in his head, he was getting just as much pleasure from this as I was. He took over again, moving my hips faster.

"I'm so close." I shook my head, fighting the sensations. "Jay, I want to feel you."

"Need you to come first, baby." He smirked up at me, pushing me down harder on his length. "There's no way I'll last long once I'm inside you, and I want to make this good for you." He slipped his fingers under the elastic of my underwear, digging into the flesh of my ass. "Tell me what you like, what you need, so I can make you come."

"Just this." It had been so long since someone cared about my pleasure. I didn't honestly know how to answer his question. "This feels so good."

I threw my head back and gyrated my hips until my core tightened.

As I came, electricity arcing through me, Jay straightened and threaded his fingers into my hair, bringing my mouth down on his and swallowing my moans.

"Get that dress off," he demanded a moment later.

Obediently, I scooted off him and stood on shaky legs. Focus fixed on him, I slowly hiked my dress up, only breaking eye contact when I pulled it over my head. He stood in front of me and mirrored the action with his shirt. God damn, I'd forgotten how amazing he looked without a shirt. He had lines that were defined between all his chest and ab muscles. Licking my lips, I reached out to touch him and brushed my fingers along his stomach and down to the waistband of his pants.

His groan gave me confidence as I worked his pants down his hips. He took over, yanking them down, along with his boxers, then discarding them. His cock was long and thick and begging to be touched.

Holding my breath, I wrapped my fingers around the base and tugged.

"Fuck," he gritted out. "Sarah, I want your hands on me,

but every time you touch me, I think I'm going to explode." He grasped my wrist and gently pulled it away. "I need to be inside you."

I pulled my bottom lip into my mouth with my teeth. I wanted that too. To move up and down his shaft while he was inside me.

He sat back down, bringing me forward to stand between his legs. "But now you have too many clothes on."

He made quick work of removing my bra, then his mouth was on my nipple, licking and sucking while he hooked his thumbs into the string of my thong and worked it over my hips and down my legs. As he lowered them, he trailed his mouth south.

He flicked his tongue against my clit, making me buck hard. Then, with his hands on my ass, he buried his face between my legs. Working his tongue back and forth, he brought me close to the peak again.

I dug my nails into his shoulders and shuddered, but just as I reached the precipice, he pulled back and grinned. Whimpering, I hung my head. I was so close, and his smirk said he knew it.

"I want to feel you come on my dick." He pulled me closer, guiding me to straddle him. "But next time, you're going to ride my face."

My breath caught. The images his words caused to flash through my mind went straight to my core, making it throb.

"You would like that, wouldn't you?" He guided my hips forward, positioning me over his cock.

"Yes." I swallowed thickly as he guided me down and stretched me. The burn and simultaneous pleasure had every nerve in my body awakening. "You're so big," I hissed.

He rotated my hips and lowered me another inch. "You can take it."

The challenge in his eyes had me smiling, but after another

inch, I dug my nails into his shoulders again and breathed through the delicious pain until I was fully seated on top of him.

"That's a good girl." His fingers bit into the flesh of my ass. "Now you need to move. Let me feel that pussy gripping my cock."

Feeling empowered, I raised up, then slowly dropped down, watching his expression.

His pupils dilated and his jaw locked tight as I picked up my pace.

"Fuck, Sarah," he growled. "Let me see those tits bounce."

His dirty words inspired me, and I arched back, sliding up and down his hard length. It was incredible, the sense of control he was giving me. He was still bracing me, but only to help me move. He let me set the pace and decide how deep I wanted to go. It made me feel free. Powerful. Sexy. Confident. All the things I hadn't felt in so long.

With one hand on my hip again, he slid the other to my stomach, then slid it low until he found my clit with his thumb and applied pressure, moving in circles.

"Right there." My core tightened, sending pleasure shooting through my body.

Abruptly, Jay locked his arms around my back, startling me, then lifted and spun us so I was on my back and he hovered over me. He pounded hard into me as my orgasm hit me with forceful waves. Two more powerful thrusts, and he groaned, emptying inside me.

Panting hard, he lowered himself onto his forearms and pressed his forehead to mine.

As I caught my breath, a variety of emotions hit me hard. I wasn't sure I'd ever experienced something so intimate, so intense. But the awe was accompanied by the fear of never experiencing it again.

Jay stood, offering me his hand. That smirk of his shooting straight to my core again.

He pulled me hard against his chest and wrapped his arms around me, resting his chin on top of my head. "Want to cuddle on the couch and watch the rest of the episode of *Brooklyn Nine-Nine* we started last night?"

I fought the surprise that bubbled up. Half of me expected him to bolt. I hated that all my shitty experiences with men had left me with such a jaded mindset. The last thing I wanted to do was let my past ruin this for me. For us.

"Sure." I sagged against him and smiled. "Can we get dressed first?"

"I'd rather keep you naked." His chest vibrated as he chuckled. "But yeah. Go put something comfortable on. I think I'll run back to my place and grab myself a pair of shorts for the night." He pulled back and pressed his lips briefly against mine.

"Okay." I picked up my discarded clothes, clutched them to my chest, and headed toward my bedroom.

Quietly, so I didn't wake Nora, I found a pair of pajama shorts and a T-shirt, and once I was dressed, I stopped in the bathroom to clean up. When I came out again, Jay had returned. We curled up together, watching TV, until I found myself yawning for the third time.

"You ready for bed?" he asked.

I nodded. "You're really staying?" I was so thankful that Nora had let me put her down in her crib, and she was still asleep. I just hoped she stayed that way.

"Yeah." He pressed his lips to my temple. "Every night if you let me."

"What?" I popped up on my elbow and stared down at him.

"You still don't get it, do you?" He shook his head, tucking my hair behind my ear. "You and Nora are it for me. This is where I want to be. Every night. Forever if you'll let me."

I laid my head on his chest. I absolutely wanted more than casual. But forever? Could I even trust my own judgment? At one time, I thought Drew loved me, wanted forever with me. Look how that turned out. I obviously sucked at seeing the red flags.

He let out a deep sigh, his chest vibrating. "I get that you might need more time to get there." Pulling me tighter into his side, he pressed his cheek to the crown of my head. "I know you're dealing with a lot. But I need you to know how I feel."

With a nod, I closed my eyes, relaxing deeper into his hold. This was the first time I'd felt truly safe and protected in the last three years.

Hope bloomed in my chest, and I prayed it wouldn't be ripped away from me once again.

Chapter Seventeen

JAY

Izzy: Are you really bringing a girl home with you today?

Angie: I'll believe it when I see it.

I WASN'T sure why they were acting surprised. Both had met a few of the girls I'd dated over the years.

Movement from next to me on the sofa had me glancing that way and smiling. Nora was asleep, though she was shifting, lashes fluttering. With a shake of my head, I typed out a quick reply.

> Me: What's with the dramatics? You guys have met plenty of the girls I've dated.

> Izzy: Yeah. But not on purpose, and you've never brought one home.

> Angie: Exactly. I only met that awful girl you dated last year because my car broke down and you brought her with you to pick me up. She bitched the entire ride about having to cut your date short.

I CRINGED. That relationship, if you could even call it that, didn't last much past that night.

As I was locking my phone—because there was no good way to respond to that last text—Sarah stepped into my line of sight. I looked up and took her in, my breath lodging in my throat. Like it did almost any time she entered a room.

"How's this?" She smoothed her hands down a navy dress that ended just above her knees.

"Perfect." I smirked.

She'd changed three times, clearly nervous. But her hair was now curled, and she'd applied makeup, so I hoped that meant she was almost ready. We were celebrating Dad's birthday, and I didn't want to be late.

More than that, though, I wanted Sarah to feel comfortable, so I wouldn't rush her out the door until she felt she was ready.

She blew out a harsh breath. "That's what you said about the jeans and sweater."

I nodded. "That was perfect too." I stood and peered down at Nora, who was still fast asleep on the couch, then approached Sarah and cupped her face. "Whatever you wear is perfect. You look gorgeous in either option, and I have no doubt my family will love you regardless of what you wear. Stop stressing."

She worried her lip and dropped her focus to my chest. "I don't have the best track record with this."

I wasn't sure exactly what she meant, but I got the idea.

"Maybe you weren't with the right guy." I pressed my lips to her forehead, and when her body sagged, I pulled her against me and wrapped my arms around her shoulders. After a moment, I leaned back to look down at her. "But tonight will be perfect. Okay?"

She nodded. "Yeah. Just wish I had your optimism sometimes."

"Relax and be yourself. It'll be fine."

After talking to my mom yesterday and then texting with my sisters, I had a feeling they were all just excited that I was bringing someone home. But I wasn't sure if mentioning that would make Sarah feel better or more nervous, so I kept quiet.

When her shoulders relaxed, relief washed over me. After confirming that she was ready to go, I scooped a still sleeping Nora off the sofa, and we headed out the door.

Almost immediately after placing Nora in the car seat, she let us know exactly how she felt about it. And a few looks over at Sarah once we were on the road told me the fussing was making her feel more stressed. So I turned up the radio and sang along with the country song. Babies liked being sung too, right?

Sarah shook her head, fighting a smile.

I reached over and nudged her thigh. "Come on, Mama. You know this one."

She chuckled but joined in, softly singing along with me.

Finally, a few songs later, Nora had stopped crying and was babbling away instead, and the tension radiating off Sarah had dissipated for the most part.

Once I parked on the street in front of my parents' small cape cod, I got Nora out of the back seat and met Sarah on the sidewalk. Grasping her hand, I gave it a squeeze. "You good?"

Shrugging, she sent me a soft smile. "As good as I'm going to get."

Hopefully she'd feel at ease as soon as she saw how excited my family was to have her here.

But it didn't dawn on me until I was inside the house how chaotic my family could be. They met us at the door, and even I was overwhelmed by their attention. Between my sisters introducing themselves to Sarah before we were even fully inside the foyer and my parents asking me how the drive over was, I worried Sarah would be ready to snatch Nora from my arms and bolt. Instead, when I stole a glance in her direction, she was smiling.

Nora, on the other hand, had her face buried into the crook of my neck and a death grip on my shirt.

"She's not even that old," Izzy directed at me, her hands on her hips.

My stomach sank. What the hell was she talking about? "What?"

"Sarah." She rolled her eyes like that was obvious. "You said she was older than you. She doesn't even *look* old."

"Jesus," I muttered. I had hoped my sister's lack of a filter was something she would grow out of. Apparently, that wasn't the case, and it didn't look like it would happen any time soon.

"Izzy," my mom and Angie scolded at the same time.

"What?" Izzy huffed. "Fine. I'll shut up now."

"Good idea," I shot back.

Sarah, thank fuck, had her lips curved inward, holding back

a laugh, and her eyes were dancing. Laughing at me and my family? I could work with.

"Come on." Angie looped her arm through Sarah's and pulled her into the living room. "You'll have to tell me how you got your hair to curl like that."

Wincing, I considered following and rescuing her before they hounded her with a whole list of questions.

"She'll be fine." My mom chuckled. "If she can handle a room full of five-year-olds all day, then thirty minutes with your sisters is nothing."

I raised one eyebrow at her. We both knew that Izzy and Angie could be far worse than kindergarteners. Izzy would spout off whatever popped into her head, and even though Angie was more careful with her words, she had a special talent for making people feel uncomfortable. And she was an expert at gathering information about a person before they even realized that was what she was doing.

But my mom was right. Sarah was handling my sisters just fine. Constant chatter about hair, makeup, and clothes came from the three of them. Even when my mom peppered Sarah with questions about how she liked her job and whether she'd considered becoming a teacher at some point, she didn't seem fazed. Ten minutes into dinner, I was feeling good about how the night was going.

"How's the new apartment?" my mom asked me as Nora, who was in Izzy's arms, held her arms out to her. "Oh, want to come sit with me now?"

Nora had warmed up quickly shortly after we arrived and seemed content visiting with each person.

My mom raised an eyebrow in my direction, reminding me that she was waiting for an answer.

"It's good." What did she want me to say? I appreciated the space and independence, but in reality, I hadn't stayed at my own place in almost a week.

"Are you even going to keep it?" Izzy asked.

"What?" My mom zeroed in on my sister. "Why wouldn't he keep it?"

I swallowed. Shit. *Here we go. Thanks, Iz.*

"'Cause he's been staying at Sarah's every night." She shrugged. "I assumed he'd want to move in with her."

Sarah's fork clattered to her plate, and I pinched my eyes closed. I really needed to stop telling Izzy anything I didn't want repeated. I didn't necessarily care whether my parents knew I was sleeping at Sarah's, but I didn't want to have that conversation right now, and I definitely didn't want to put Sarah on the spot.

"You know what they say about assuming, right?" I narrowed my eyes at Izzy, silently begging her to shut up.

Wide-eyed, she scanned the large oak table, at least attempting to read the room before she sighed and went back to eating her food.

"Have I ever told you about the time I had to clear an apartment building with a python loose in it?" my dad interjected.

We all groaned in unison. Yes, we'd heard this story at least a dozen times. I was grateful for the change of topic, but I wasn't sure one of my dad's stories was any better. Even if it was one of my favorites.

"A bunch of men who run into burning buildings every day afraid of a snake." My dad shook his head, chuckling. "In fairness, not being able to see more than a foot in front of us made us all jumpy any time we saw movement."

Sarah cringed but was totally engrossed in the story.

After he'd finished, he launched into question after question about how Angie's last year of college was going. She was getting a BS in computer engineering and had already applied for several internships in Asheville.

"Everyone ready for cake?" my mom asked.

"Is that even a question?" My dad tilted his head with a smirk plastered on his face. "I'm always ready for cake."

I took the cue that our dinner dishes needed to be cleared and leaned over to whisper in Sarah's ear. "You good?"

She nodded and then sent me a smile.

Standing, I started to collect our plates, and as I headed for the kitchen, my mom handed Nora back to Izzy and followed me.

I rinsed dishes and loaded the dishwasher while my mom got out a serving tray and placed it on the marble countertop next to me.

"Sarah's great." She dropped the forks onto the tray, opened the cabinet in front of her, and pulled out a handful of small plates.

"I know." If there was a but to her statement, I wasn't sure I wanted to hear it.

In my periphery, she paused, studying me, until I gave in and turned to face her.

She sighed. "I can tell you care about her, and I'm thrilled you found someone. But just don't rush things."

"I'm not." I locked my jaw, thinking about Izzy's comment earlier. "I'm not giving up my apartment and moving in with her." *Not yet*, at least.

"You tend to dive headfirst into things. Just remember that there's a child involved, and it's only been a month. It's important to be sure before you make any big decisions."

I was sure of my feelings for Sarah. But I got what my mom was saying. Sarah still had her doubts, or rather, insecurities, and she had a lot on her plate with the whole Drew situation. So I had no plans to rush her into something she wasn't ready for. I also understood what a commitment of any kind would mean. For Sarah, for Nora, even for me.

I nodded. "Roger that."

She smiled at the words my dad and I always used to let her know we heard her and understood.

A few minutes later, I took my seat next to Sarah. I put my arm around her and pulled her closer, pressing my lips to her temple.

I tried my hardest throughout the rest of the night and on the drive back home to not overthink what my mom had said. But I failed. Was I rushing into things?

All I knew was that lying in bed with Sarah in my arms later that night felt like the surest thing I'd ever known.

Chapter Eighteen

JAY

"Maybe I need two." I organized the last of the tools into their spot in the compartment on the side of the firetruck before turning back to Owen. I'd promised my mom I wouldn't rush things with Sarah, but I also refused to sit around and do nothing about the Drew issue. "One for her and one for me."

"Huh?" Owen's brows pulled together as he added supplies to one of the drawers.

"It isn't like I can log into her app." That was going a little too far. As my mom had pointed out, it had only been a month. Sarah probably wouldn't be ready to give me access to a security camera. "That would be weird. I'll have to point my camera at her door."

Easy solution. I'd install one, but make sure it's aimed at her door. Since I couldn't be with them all the time, I needed to do something to protect them. I needed to make sure they were both safe.

"Dude, that's kinda stalkery too." He chuckled.

"Are you kidding me?" I huffed. "I need to do something. Wouldn't you do the same if it were Cece?"

"Yeah, of course." He shrugged. "But I pretty much forced Cece to let me move in with her, so she already knows I'm over-the-top."

He wasn't lying there. Maybe I couldn't be with my girls all the time, but this way, I could make sure no one who shouldn't be near her apartment was loitering.

"Maybe I'm over-the-top too, then." I'd rather be overly cautious than risk their safety.

"Not typically." Owen cocked an eyebrow. "But I'm taking it that Sarah is important to you."

Yeah. The most important person in my life. Owen was one of my closest friends, but if he was about to list off the reasons why she shouldn't be, I might punch him.

"She is." I stood to my full height and crossed my arms over my chest.

Rather than give me shit, he smirked. "Good."

Asshole. I shook my head and turned away from him.

He understood exactly where I was coming from. He would do whatever it took to protect the woman he loved.

And so would I.

Chapter Nineteen

SARAH

I STARED out the passenger side window with a smile plastered on my face. The last few nights had been perfect. Our normal routine wasn't anything exciting. Just dinner and football or a show. But after Nora went down for the night, we'd get lost in each other.

Jay brushed a thumb back and forth along the top of mine, the subtle movement making my stomach flutter. A sigh left my lips.

Even though I hadn't gotten another text this week, he

insisted on staying the night. Which was fine with me, and Nora was excited each morning when she woke up, standing in her crib, reaching toward us.

It felt like a miracle. She'd gradually been going down easier over the last few weeks and had begun sleeping through the night in her crib. And the nights Jay put her down always went the smoothest.

"Are you nervous?" Jay's question cut through my thoughts.

"Not really." I shrugged. "My parents are excited to meet you."

I guess I was a little anxious about what my mom would think. She was a good judge of character. Time after time, she'd warned me about red flags in my shitty relationships that I'd completely missed. Nerves fluttered through me. Was this just another time I was being blind?

I didn't think so.

Nora hadn't stopped babbling since we pulled out of the lot. But Jay had also not stopped having a conversation, however one-sided it was, with her. Who did that?

Stomach fluttering, I studied the man sitting in the driver's seat talking nonsense with my one-year-old in the back seat. There was no denying it. I was falling for this selfless, protective man. The way he fussed over my daughter and the way, with just a look, he made me feel like I was the only thing he could see, was slowly healing my battered heart.

He turned my way and smiled.

I had no doubt he would walk over burning coals to get to someone he loved.

I swallowed hard. Maybe I wasn't being blind. Or maybe Jay deserved better than a thirtysomething single mom with way too much baggage.

But almost two hours later, my mom hadn't said a word or given me any clue that she didn't approve. In fact, both my parents seemed smitten with Jay. And really, who wouldn't be? That boyish smirk of his worked not only on Nora and me, but on anyone it was aimed at.

As I was pouring lemonade into my glass, my mom stepped into the kitchen. Tensing, I peered through the opening above the sink that led into my parents' living room. Jay and my dad roared as the commentator on TV confirmed a fumble. I should've known the two would bond over football.

I spun toward my mom, one eyebrow slightly raised.

"You okay?" she asked.

"Please tell me you think he's great."

She smiled. "Do you think he's great?"

I huffed. I loved my mom, but I did not have time for her reverse psychology crap tonight.

"Of course. I think he's amazing. But I've been blind to red flags before." I sucked in air, then forced out the last of my thoughts. "So please, for the love of God, tell me I'm not wrong this time."

"Oh, honey." She pulled me into a hug. "I can't promise you that he won't break your heart, but no, I don't think you're wrong for thinking he's amazing." She pulled back to look at me. "And I think he feels the same."

"Why do you say that?"

"Because all night, his attention has been fixed on either you or Nora."

I glanced back into the living room, meeting Jay's gaze. The smirk he shot back had my body doing stupid things.

"He's really good with her," I whispered as my one-year-old giggled from where she was balanced on his knee.

Her smile was slow. "He is."

There was a but coming. Dammit. Heart in my throat, I studied her, waiting.

"But just make sure he's as amazing with you as he is with her."

My stomach twisted. It was important that my potential life partner cherish Nora the way I did. But no, that wasn't the only reason my heart soared. He looked at me with so much affection, and his touch made me feel safe, loved. Even the way he cared for Nora showed his affection and dedication to me. He was obviously smitten with Nora, but he also understood that by taking care of her, he was taking care of me. Like occupying her while I cooked dinner or putting her to bed so I didn't feel guilty leaving her there crying for me.

The thoughts swirled for the rest of the evening. Even after he carried Nora out and put her into her seat and we were in the car heading home. Even after he continued to be patient with me every time I said he didn't have to do something. He would just cup my cheek and remind me for the hundredth time that he knew, but that he *wanted* to.

Chapter Twenty

JAY

I PROPPED myself up against the wall, one ankle crossed over the other, and watched, entranced by this gorgeous woman working in her kitchen. She subconsciously did a little booty shake as she washed the dishes.

These carefree moments, when she wasn't stressing or worrying about all the things that loomed over her, were rare, and I couldn't help but soak them in. I'd offered to put Nora to bed because it was easier on Sarah. Although Nora had been going down better, it was clear that it still hurt Sarah to leave Nora in her crib if she was fussing.

As I came up behind her, she startled, but quickly, she relaxed back into my chest.

I understood now why she startled so easily sometimes. But would that ever go away?

"So did I get the parental approval?"

"My dad gave you his favorite beer." She chuckled. "He only does that for people he likes."

"Yeah, but he asked if I was old enough to have one first."

She spun, and her mouth fell open. "He did what?"

"I thought it was hilarious." I shrugged. "Your dad speaks my language."

Lips turning down, she lowered her head and focused on the floor between us.

I gripped her chin with my thumb and forefinger, gently raising her face so I could look her in the eyes.

"What is it?"

"People will wonder why a hot young guy like you is dating a thirty-one-year-old single mom."

My heart clenched at the sadness in her tone. I didn't give a shit about what people thought. "You have it backward. They're all going to wonder what the blond bombshell is doing with the young idiot."

Her only response was a sigh.

I tucked a stray strand of hair behind her ear. "You think I'm hot?"

She rolled her eyes. "You know you are. Don't act like you don't."

I trailed one hand up her side and brushed my fingers along the underside of her breast, dying to get my mouth around her nipples. She was so damn responsive when I lavished them with attention. I yanked on the tie that held her wrap dress in place, and when her breath hitched in response, I couldn't hide my smirk.

"I like hearing you say it." I untied the inside string, then stepped back to take in her hourglass figure clad in a silky dark purple bra and panty set.

She slid the fabric of the dress off her shoulders, letting it fall to a puddle on the floor. The slight pout of her lips and dilated eyes told me she was enjoying this.

"Do you doubt how sexy I think you are?" she asked, head tilted to one side.

I shrugged, biting back a grin. "Maybe you should remind me."

Her hands disappeared behind her back, and a second later, her bra joined her dress on the floor. My dick grew painfully hard. Her full breasts were screaming for my attention, and my hands twitched as her fingers latched on to the waistband of the purple thong that covered where I wanted my mouth to be. But I kept my feet planted in place, thoroughly enjoying the torturous show.

My mouth went dry as she slid the scrap of fabric down her legs.

"Here," she said as she tossed it toward me. "See how wet I am for you."

Fuck me. I didn't need to see anything to know she needed me just as much as I needed her, but I brought the damp material to my nose, breathing in her arousal, then I let it fall to the floor.

"I think I need to see for myself." I was moving toward her then, and our bodies crashed together as our mouths fused. In one fluid movement, I slid my hand between her legs. Lips trailing down the column of her throat, then lower, I mumbled "so wet" against the supple skin of her breasts, my fingers exploring and teasing, just barely touching the spot that I knew would send her flying.

"Jay," she breathed out.

I circled one nipple with my tongue, and she gripped the hair at the back of my head, holding me against her.

"I need..." Her hips gyrated, and she arched into me. "Please."

The groan that escaped her as I moved my fingers away from her pussy was filled with so much annoyance, I couldn't help but smile against her skin. I had no intention of letting her come on my hand.

Slipping my hands lower, I grabbed tightly onto the globes of her ass and lifted her into my arms, spinning and setting her on the island.

"Lean back, baby. I want you to come on my tongue."

With a smile, she did as I asked, leaning back on her elbows and lifting her feet so her heels were balanced on the edge. I held her legs open wide with my palms, taking in her glistening pussy.

She shifted onto one elbow and brought her fingers down, moving them in a circle around her clit. I tipped my head back and groaned. That was the hottest thing I'd ever seen. As she continued to touch herself, I couldn't look away. My dick begged to be let out so he could join in on the fun. But he would just have to wait.

"Keep that up." Stepping back, I grabbed the material of my shirt. Then I yanked it over my head and discarded it on the floor with her clothing. With my focus locked on her, I unsnapped the button of my jeans.

Licking her lips and drinking me in as I pushed my jeans and boxers to the floor, she picked up her pace, moving her fingers in tight circles.

She threw her head back, moaning. "Jay, I'm so close."

"Don't you dare come yet." I swatted her hand away and leaned down, covering her clit with my mouth.

I flicked my tongue back and forth across her sensitive skin, making her buck against me, until her muscles contracted and she was moaning my name. Once she'd fallen over that edge, I slowed my movements, letting her ride out her orgasm.

When she'd come back down, I peppered kisses along her lower belly and then up to her breasts, where I teased one nipple, then the other. "So perfect," I mumbled as she was racked with aftershocks. Damn, I couldn't wait another moment to be inside her.

Pulling her back into my arms, I lifted her, guiding her legs to wrap around my hips. Then I spun toward the wall behind me and pinned her against it with my body. Panting and desperate, I lined up the tip of my cock with her entrance, then I slowly lowered her.

"Fuck, baby," I groaned as her hot, wet heat surrounded me. "You feel too good."

"So good." She ran her fingers tenderly through my hair.

I held her gaze as I began to move. Slowly, in and out of her, wanting to savor as much as I could before I couldn't hold back any longer.

Our breaths mingled between us as we held eye contact. This was a first for me. Usually, sex was just sex. But this felt like so much more. More intimate. Sensual. Three words moved to the tip of my tongue, and I had to bite them back. The last thing I wanted to do was ruin this moment by over-whelming her with my feelings.

"Kiss me," she whispered, her tone desperate, like maybe she was feeling the strong emotions that swirled around us too.

I covered her mouth with mine, brushing my lips gently back and forth. She matched my movements, but a moment later, she broke the kiss and dropped her head back against the wall. Her pussy gripped my cock tightly, signaling that she was close again.

"Sarah, look at me." I slammed up into her. "I want to watch you."

Opening her eyes, she zeroed in on me.

"Jay, I—" She searched my face, then quickly glanced away.

"Sarah, baby." I brushed my lips against her cheek and pulled back. "Let me see you."

She was feeling the same intense emotions I was, that was obvious, but I needed her to stay with me and in the moment.

Mouth open wide, she focused on me again. Two more thrusts, and waves of pleasure shot through her. Her pussy squeezed my hard length until I followed her over the edge, exploding inside her.

I dropped my forehead to rest against hers and breathed deeply. Giving us both a minute to come back down from that intense experience.

And I couldn't hold back telling her how I felt as the emotion hit me hard in the chest. "I love you, Sarah."

She pulled back slightly and searched my face, the corners of her mouth lifting into a smile.

"I love you too."

Later that night, once we climbed into bed, we quietly made love again, whispering how we felt into the darkness that surrounded us as we came together before drifting off the sleep.

Chapter Twenty-One

JAY

I LAID BACK on the sofa in the common area of the firehouse with one arm tucked behind my head. In my other hand, my phone buzzed.

Sarah: We just got up. About to make breakfast.

I'D LEFT for work at five this morning. While I was getting ready, Sarah had brought Nora to bed with her, and the sight of the two of them cuddled up together made me ache to stay with them.

I glanced around the firehouse. A few of the guys were eating breakfast while the others were finishing a game of rummy. This place used to be my escape. Where I'd chill until those alarms went off. Now it didn't feel that way. Now, it felt like a place where I had to go through the motions, power through the hours, until I could be where I wanted to be most.

I shot Sarah a text back, smiling as I did.

> Me: Don't tell me you're making waffles again.

THREE DOTS APPEARED and disappeared in rapid succession. I chuckled. Ruffling her feathers by teasing her about her latest mishap was way too much fun.

> Me: Should I prepare the guys to head over?

> Sarah: 😶

> Sarah: Between that night I burned the chicken and then leaving the waffle griddle on, it might not be a bad idea. I'm a fire hazard.

THE ALARMS BLARED LOUDLY, and I jumped up off the sofa, then shot Sarah another text.

> Me: Going on a call. Don't burn anything. I'll text when we're back at the house.

WHAT SHOULD HAVE BEEN a simple call to put out a fire turned into pulling a handful of teenagers out of the old boathouse that was ablaze. Apparently, they'd been using it as a place to lay low away from the adults in their lives. To make matters worse, the place was close to the tree line, and we had to work to keep the flames under control so the forest didn't catch fire too.

It was hours before we were back at the firehouse. Some of the guys started drills, burning off the excess adrenaline, and some crashed on their cots. I was always the one who ran for coffee and pastries after a call like this. Because what better way to perk up than with a coffee and some sugar? It wasn't a big deal, but it was something that I could do for the guys.

But before I headed out, I had more important things to do.

> Me: We're back. How are my girls doing?

JUST AS I HIT SEND, a notification popped up. It was from the Ring camera app I'd installed after mounting the camera outside my door last week. I clicked on it, and as the video loaded, my stomach sank. Shit. No way I wouldn't recognize the greased-back hair. What the hell was he doing outside of Sarah's apartment?

"Fuck" flew from my mouth, causing the guys nearby to whip their heads in my direction. "I need to call Sarah."

I paced the length of the small sitting area as the phone rang once and then went straight to voicemail.

"What's wrong?"

Ignoring Owen's question, I tried again. When she still didn't answer, I switched back over to the app. But it was too late to warn her. Drew was disappearing into Sarah's apartment. Fear and anger coursed through me. If he hurt them... No. They had to be okay. I couldn't lose them.

"I gotta go." I turned and almost barreled into Owen.

He stopped me with his hands on my shoulders. "What's going on?"

"Drew just broke into Sarah's apartment." The words stuck in my throat as I tried to shove out of his grasp.

"Dude, stop." His fingers tightened on my arm.

"No fucking way." I glared. "They need me."

"Not alone. We all go. Come on." He waved at the guys around us as I pushed past him and headed for the stairs that led down to the bay. "No one goes after our family."

Though terror still gripped me, my heart skipped as my team headed down the stairs to help me protect my girls. It was something I could give Sarah. She didn't get just me, but my family. My parents and sisters, and my work family.

Less than five minutes later, we were loaded up, and Logan was turning on the sirens as he maneuvered the rig out onto the street. Owen was on the phone with Dylan while I tried Sarah once more.

"God dammit," I yelled as her voicemail picked up again. *Please, God, don't let anything happen to them.*

If I hadn't already been 100 percent sure that they were my future, it would have been more than obvious to me now. Never in my life had I been this scared.

Chapter Twenty-Two

SARAH

CONFUSION SWAMPED me as I pulled into the parking lot.

Crap. Did I leave the waffle iron on again?

I parked the car and got out, surveying the scene.

I caught sight of Owen first. He saw me at the same moment and nodded in my direction. Then Jay, who was standing beside him, turned, relief flooding his features. A second later, he was moving toward me.

Between the fire truck, ambulance, and multiple police cars, whatever was going on couldn't have been good.

"What's wrong? Is there a fire?" I asked when he was close enough.

"No." He pulled me into his muscular chest and wrapped his arms around me. "Where were you?"

"At the grocery."

His shoulders relaxed, and his whole body deflated. "I tried calling."

"Sorry. Nora was being difficult. I think she might be coming down with something."

He pulled back and peered into the back seat.

I shook my head. "She's asleep now, but I was trying to be quick in the store and get her back home. So I didn't really look at my phone."

He pulled me back against him.

Heart still beating quickly, I tilted my head up. "Are you going to tell me what's going on?"

"Don't freak out."

Too late for that. Just his demeanor told me I wasn't going to like what he had to say.

But I nodded anyway. "Okay..."

"Drew's in your apartment."

"*What?*" I half squeaked and half yelled, pulling back.

He smirked, though his eyes were still filled with concern. "You said you wouldn't freak out, remember?"

I huffed. That was before he told me my abusive ex was in my apartment.

"It's okay. Officers just went in to arrest him."

Sighing, I rested my cheek against his chest, doing my best not to let fear overwhelm me. I was safe. Nora was safe.

We stayed like that until another police car pulled up next to us a few minutes later.

Dylan climbed out and approached us. "You okay?" His jaw was tense as he scanned me, likely looking for injuries.

Memories from that night almost two years ago flooded

me. The ER, the fear of losing Nora, giving the police a statement and having to recount what Drew had done.

Pulling myself out of the doom spiral I'd fallen into, I pressed my lips together and nodded. "Yes. I'm fine."

He gave me a tight nod. Was he, too, thinking of that night? He had been one of the officers on the scene that day.

Commotion at the front of our building drew my attention. Dylan strode that direction when the officers appeared; each was holding one of Drew's arms where they were restrained behind his back as he bucked against their hold and yelled manically.

Jay stepped into my line of sight, pulling me into his embrace once again.

"I was so scared," he mumbled against the top of my head.

"Huh?" Too many thoughts were swirling around my head to comprehend his words.

God. What if Nora and I had been in the apartment? Would Drew still have broken in? I probably didn't want to know.

Jay pulled back, cupping my face with his hands and tilting my head up to look at him. "I thought you guys were in there when I saw Drew breaking in."

The anguished look he now wore stabbed painfully at my heart.

"I don't know what I'd do if anything happened to either one of you." His voice cracked as he spoke.

Grasping his wrists, I shook my head. "I'm sorry."

He pulled me back into his chest, wrapping his arms tightly around me.

"We're okay, though. Everything's okay." I clung tightly to him.

But then his words registered, and I frowned as I processed them.

"How did you see him?"

His body tightened as he winced. "My Ring camera."

I looked from him to the building, trying to understand. Our apartments were next to each other. Ring cameras typically pointed in front of a person's door, not to the left or right. So how in the world?

"I don't understand."

"I might have installed my camera so it pointed at your door." One corner of his mouth lifted, and he ducked his head, sheepish. "Apparently, I'm over-the-top when it comes to the people I love."

Jesus. But I couldn't even be mad, nor was I surprised that this protective man had gone above and beyond to make sure we were safe.

With a sigh, I burrowed into his chest and held him tight.

"You're not mad?"

"No." A tear ran down my cheek. "No one has ever been over-the-top for me."

He chuckled into my hair and kissed the top of my head.

"I'll always be over-the-top for you."

Chapter Twenty-Three

JAY

THERE WAS NO BETTER way to start off the new year than with the woman I loved in my arms. Sarah disconnected the call with her lawyer and set the phone on the nightstand, then snuggled in close with her head on my chest.

"What'd he say?"

Not only had Drew broken into Sarah's apartment, but he had resisted arrest and violated his probation. He'd also been armed and carrying the disposable cell that he'd been using to send those texts.

"Drew will more than likely be going away for a long time and won't be my problem anymore."

"*Our* problem."

"Huh?"

"You and me." I brushed my hand up and down her arm. "*Our* problem."

She nodded. "Right. *Our* problem."

The moment Drew had been shoved into the back of that police car, the dark cloud that had been hanging over us had disappeared. In those first couple of weeks after the incident, she'd still needed occasional reminders that she and Nora were my future and that I liked taking care of them. That here with them was where I wanted to be and I had no intention of going anywhere. She was stuck with me.

"I'm giving my apartment up at the end of this month."

She popped up, eyes wide. "What?"

Even though I expected the dramatic response, it still had me smiling. I prayed she was brave enough to embrace the change, because this was where I belonged.

"Yeah, I'm always here anyway."

I literally couldn't remember the last time I'd spent the night at my place.

She smiled. "Didn't you just take over the lease from Owen in October?"

I shrugged. "I don't need it anymore."

She hummed. "Then when my lease expires in March, we should probably look into upgrading to a two-bedroom."

My heart soared at her easy tone. "That's my girl."

She rolled her eyes and chuckled, then snuggled back into my side.

Exactly where she belonged.

Epilogue

JAY

GIGGLES ERUPTED from the dance floor, and I smiled at the scene. Nora held the young toddler's hands as the two danced in a circle. She was so good with Owen's daughter, and it was obvious that she would be the best big sister when the time came. And now that Sarah and I were married, I was hoping we could make that happen in the next year.

Nora caught my attention and waved excitedly. She was getting so big. Three was creeping up faster than I expected.

"Congratulations," Owen said as he stepped up next to me. "How does it feel to be an old married guy now?"

"You might be old." I smirked. "I'm still the youngest guy in the firehouse."

The guys still continued to give me crap about it.

"How do you feel about that?" He tipped his head toward Logan, who was standing at the bar talking to Izzy.

"He better not be buying her a drink." I narrowed my eyes. "She's not twenty-one yet."

And I didn't care that she would be in only a few months.

Owen chuckled. "That wasn't what I meant—"

"Dada." Grace waddled toward Owen. "Dada."

Owen met her halfway and scooped the young girl up into his arms.

"Daddy." Nora skipped toward me and grabbed my hand. "Come dance with me."

Drew had refused to sign away his parental rights, but we were holding out hope that he would sometime before he was released in twelve years. If not, it didn't matter. Nora would always be my daughter. I didn't need a piece of paper to prove it.

"Any time," I said as I held her hands and helped her step up onto my toes.

After a few minutes, Sarah and Cece made their way back onto the dance floor. It was nice that the two of them had gotten close. Even Cece's friend Kelly got along great with Sarah, and the three of them had become inseparable.

I scooped Nora up, nestling her into the crook of one arm, and wrapped my free arm around Sarah, pulling her close.

As I drank in the moment, my heart soared. There was nothing better than dancing with my girls.

Ready for more Half Moon Lake firefighters?
Preorder the first two books in the Half Moon Lake Heroes:
The Red Line!
Playing with Fire
Out of the Fire

More By A J Ranney

Half Moon Lake Series:

Always Yours (book 1)

Wishing to be Yours (book 1.5)

Impossibly Yours (book 2)

Imperfectly Yours (book 3)

Bravely Yours (book 3.5)

Recklessly Yours (book 4)

Half Moon Lake Heroes: The Red Line

Bravely Yours (book 0.5)

Playing with Fire

Out of the Fire

WRITING AS GRACIE YORK

Goldilocks and the Grumpy Bear

Tumbling Head Over Heels

Along Came The Girl

Peter Pumpkined Out

Back Together Again

Note from the Author

Dear Reader,

THANK YOU for reading *Bravely Yours*. I've been waiting for this one since the day I started writing Always Yours and struggled to make Sarah a true villain. She spoke to me in profound ways. It took me lots of frogs before I met my happy ever after. And to protect my kids? I'd do anything. So thank you for letting me share this one with you!

Now I'm excited to give Hattie Williams her happy ever after! And then the rest of the guys at Half Moon Lake Fire Department!

I appreciate each and every one of you. It's only because people like you read our books that authors like me get to publish them.

Check out my website for bonus content and stay up to date with latest releases.

Love,
AJ Ranney
www.ajranney.com

Acknowledgments

Like always, I need to thank my husband first. He has been one of my biggest cheerleaders, is always willing to listen to what I write, and has done bedtime with the kids more times than I probably realize. I appreciate your eagerness to help me when I'm stuck and your willingness to let me read to you.

And then to my kids, who are always curious about what Mommy is writing. And yes, you still need to wait until you're eighteen to read them. But by then I doubt you'd want to!

Jenn, I know you're sick of my stories by the time we get to this part! Regardless, thank you for dealing with my constant *how do I fix this?* questions and talking me down every time I'm ready to burn everything I write. You're always willing to read and edit multiple times, hold my hand when I need it, and tell me to just do it when I need that too. But above everything you've done, your friendship has meant the world to me.

A HUGE thank you to my author friends who have supported me in so many ways, whether through encouragement or reading my stuff: Annie Charme, Kat Long, Jenni Bara, Brittanee Nicole, Daphne Elliot, Kristin Lee, Amanda Zook and many more!

Also to all my beta readers: thank you for always willing to read and give feedback!

Amy, thank you for being patient as I struggled time and time again. For helping me with Tiktok, graphics, getting organized and just being an amazing friend!

Beth, thank you for being so flexible, your edits, and the millions of questions, hand holding, and messages.

Holly, as always, thank you for being my sister, even if not by blood—and to my mom and mother-in-law: You have been so supportive throughout every step of this crazy journey!

And finally, thank you to the rest of my friends and family who have helped or supported me. I used to think it took a village to raise little humans, and that still holds true, but it also takes a village to write and publish a book!

About the Author

A.J. Ranney lives in Maryland with her ever-growing zoo, including two kids, two cats, an attention-loving dog, a bunny, a cricket-eating lizard, and her lovable, well-meaning husband. She likes to leave the chaos of her real world behind and lose herself in a steamy romance novel. Her passion for reading romance prompted her writing journey, leading her to create relatable happily ever afters that come from her own dreams and experiences.

She loves coffee, sushi, wine, and her family. Not necessarily in that order. Her inner peace comes from the water, always relating to her zodiac sign, the Pisces. It's no wonder the small town she created in her stories is situated on a lake.

Follow Me

Come be apart of my Facebook Group.
AJ's Book Nook

Find me on social media:
Instagram.com/a.j.ranney
Facebook.com/ajranney19
tiktok.com/@ajranney3
Goodreads.com/AJ Ranney
http://www.ajranney.com